◆HARLEQUIN SELECTS

SHIPMENT 1

Sierra's Homecoming by Linda Lael Miller
Mountain Sheriff by B.J. Daniels
That One Night by Brenda Novak
Grayson by Delores Fossen
The Valentine Two-Step by RaeAnne Thayne
Whispering Rock by Robyn Carr

SHIPMENT 2

The McKettrick Way by Linda Lael Miller
Dancing in the Moonlight by RaeAnne Thayne
Day of Reckoning by B.J. Daniels
The More I Love You by Brenda Novak
Dade by Delores Fossen
A Love Like This by Diana Palmer

SHIPMENT 3

The House on Cannon Beach by RaeAnne Thayne
Branded by B.J. Daniels
Nate by Delores Fossen
Taylor's Temptation by Suzanne Brockmann
Never Say Die by Tess Gerritsen
A Husband to Remember by Lisa Jackson
The Marriage Charm by Linda Lael Miller

SHIPMENT 4

Heart of the Eagle by Lindsay McKenna
Lassoed by B.J. Daniels
Kade by Delores Fossen
Whistleblower by Tess Gerritsen
A Twist of Fate by Lisa Jackson
Welcome to Serenity by Sherryl Woods

DADE

USA TODAY BESTSELLING AUTHOR
DELORES FOSSEN

ISBN-13: 978-1-335-40579-1

Dade
First published in 2011. This edition published in 2021.
Copyright © 2011 by Delores Fossen

This edition published by arrangement with Harlequin Books S.A.

For questions and comments about the quality of this book, please contact us at CustomerService@Harlequin.com.

Harlequin Enterprises ULC
22 Adelaide St. West, 40th Floor
Toronto, Ontario M5H 4E3, Canada
www.Harlequin.com

Printed in U.S.A.

Delores Fossen, a *USA TODAY* bestselling author, has sold over seventy-five novels, with millions of copies of her books in print worldwide. She's received a Booksellers' Best Award and an RT Reviewers' Choice Best Book Award. She was also a finalist for a prestigious RITA® Award. You can contact the author through her website at deloresfossen.com.

Chapter 1

Kayla Brennan sure didn't look like a killer.

That was Deputy Sheriff Dade Ryland's first thought when his glare landed on the blonde who was running down the staircase. His second thought went in a different direction.

A *bad* one.

More specifically to her dark purple dress that hugged every curve of her body. Real curves. Something that always got his attention even when it shouldn't.

Like now, for instance.

Sex and Kayla Brennan shouldn't be occupying the same side of his brain.

He'd seen her before, of course, from a distance. Just over a year ago at the Silver Creek sheriff's office where she was being questioned about her husband's suspicious fatal car accident. That day Dade watched her from the doorway of his office. But she'd been pregnant then and had hidden those spicy blue eyes behind a pair of designer sunglasses. She'd shown no emotion of any kind.

Unlike now.

He saw just a flash of fear before she closed down. That pretty face became a rock-hard wall.

Dade cleared his throat and kicked up his glare a notch, hoping both would give him an attitude adjustment. It did. But then it wasn't hard to remember that this curvy blonde might be partly responsible for the death of someone he loved.

"I heard the doorbell," Kayla announced. She paused on the bottom step when she spotted Dade in the doorway, and her attention flew in the direction of the other man in the foyer. "Who's he?" she demanded.

Because Kayla apparently didn't recognize him, Dade tapped the badge clipped to his rawhide belt. "*He* has a name, and it's Deputy Sheriff Dade Ryland." He nudged the other man aside and stepped into the foyer so he could close the door.

Her left eyebrow rose, and her gaze slipped back to Dade. "You're a deputy?" She didn't wait for him to answer. "You look more outlaw than lawman."

Yeah, he got that a lot, but Dade wasn't about to let Kayla get away with the observation. "You'd know all about outlaws, wouldn't you?"

She flinched a little. Just enough to make Dade wonder exactly how raw that nerve was he'd hit.

Her flinch quickly turned to a scalpel-sharp glare, and she was almost as good at that particular expression as he was. "What are you doing in my house?"

House. That was a loose term for what was actually the Texas-sized mansion on the outskirts of his hometown of Silver Creek. A mansion she'd inherited when her husband had been killed. Dade had been raised nearby in a big ranch house with sixteen rooms, but he was betting the Brennan place was double that size.

The same probably went for Kayla's pocketbook, although Dade had some one-upmanship on her in that particular department. His family had earned their money through hard, back-breaking, honest work on the ranch. Kayla had married her millions, and those millions were as dirty as she no doubt was.

"I'm here on official business," Dade informed her. He glanced at the bald, gorilla-sized man who moved a few steps away. Dade knew his name was Kenneth Mitchell.

Kayla's so-called bodyguard.

Probably more like a hired gun as dirty as the woman paying his salary, and that's why Dade kept his hand on his gun tucked in his shoulder holster.

"The deputy says you're in his protective custody," Kenneth relayed to Kayla. His bulky body strained against his black suit, just as the muscles in his face strained against his skin.

She studied Dade, her eyes narrowing. "How did you know I was here? I led everyone to believe that I'd be at my house in San Antonio."

Dade shrugged, figuring the answer was obvious. "The district attorney, Winston Calhoun, called the sheriff and told him."

The way she pulled in her breath let him know that the answer had not been so obvious to her after all. "Mr. Calhoun assured me that he would keep my whereabouts a secret."

Dade tipped his head to the badge again. "He didn't exactly announce it to the press. He told me because you're in my protective custody."

Her eyes narrowed even more. "Protective custody?" she repeated. "How do you figure that?"

Dade walked closer to her. "Easy. You're the state's material witness, and the D.A. wants you alive long enough to testify against your father-in-law."

There it was in a nutshell, but that didn't begin to cover what Dade wanted from this woman. Yes, he wanted her to testify against her late-husband's scummy father, Charles Brennan. He wanted her to take the stand and spill her guts about the extortion and murders that Brennan had committed. While she was at it, Dade wanted to know if Brennan had killed his own son—Kayla's husband.

But those were just the icing.

What Dade really wanted her to admit on the stand was that she'd had some part in another crime.

Ellie's murder.

Dade had to take a deep breath as those memories crashed through him.

Ellie hadn't been just his sister-in-law and his twin brother's wife. Dade had loved her as deeply as he did his blood family. Kayla Brennan and her scumbag father-in-law were going to pay for killing Ellie.

"Don't worry," Kayla said with a sappy sweetness that couldn't be genuine. "I didn't come out of hiding just to let someone silence me."

No, but Kayla had come out of hiding after nearly a year. So she could testify, she'd told the D.A. But Dade wondered if there was more to it than that. He knew the D.A. had been trying to contact her for months, and she hadn't responded.

Until three hours ago.

Then, Kayla had called D.A. Winston Calhoun and told him that she would testify against her father-in-law in an extortion and racketeering trial. A trial that could send Charles Brennan to jail for several decades.

Hardly the death sentence Dade wanted for him.

However, Dade was willing to bet that Brennan had no plans to spend one minute behind bars, much less a decade. And he probably wouldn't. From what Dade had read, the case was weak at best, and witnesses kept backing out or disappearing.

But now Kayla had arrived on the scene.

Dade couldn't believe Kayla had doing her civic duty in mind. No, this was probably some kind of revenge move to get back at her father-in-law. No honor among thieves in the Brennan clan.

"I wasn't worried about you," Dade corrected. "Just doing a job I was ordered to do." And he had indeed been ordered by not just the sheriff, who was his brother, but by the D.A. Kayla was a star witness in every sense of the word, and a lot of people wanted her alive.

She made a sound of sarcastic amusement and breezed past him to head toward the double front doors. "I'll stay alive so I can testify, and I don't need you or anyone else in your family to protect me. That's why I hired Kenneth."

Dade stared at her. Well, he stared at her backside anyway because she was already walking away from him. Her low thin heels made delicate clicks on the veiny marble floor.

"I don't care how many guns you hire,"

Dade informed her. "You're still in my protective custody."

Kayla stopped and glanced at him from over her shoulder. The corner of her rose-tinged mouth lifted just a fraction, but it wasn't a smile on her face. "Protective custody, you say? Right. Those two words don't go together when it comes to you or any member of your family. The Rylands hate me."

Dade didn't deny it. "We have reason to hate you."

"No." She huffed, causing a wisp of her hair to move slightly. "You have reason to hate someone for your sister-in-law's murder, but I didn't have anything to do with it."

"Got proof of that?"

"Do you have proof to the contrary?" she fired right back at him.

He leaned in a little. "If I did, your butt would be in jail right now."

Another smirk. A short-lived one. She turned away so that he couldn't see her face. Her head lowered slightly. "Well, because I'm here and not in the Silver Creek jail, you obviously have no proof. So you can leave."

"I wish." Dade went closer while keeping an eye on Kayla's bodyguard. "Nothing would make me happier than to walk out that door and leave you to deal with the wolves, but I have my orders."

"You can take your orders and get out." She reached for the doorknob, but Dade snagged her wrist with his left hand.

The wrist snag obviously didn't sit well with her bodyguard because he reached for his gun. Dade reached for his, too.

"Stop this!" Kayla practically yelled. She jerked her hand away from Dade and shook her head. "Please," she said. Her voice was softer now but edged with the nerves that were right beneath her skin. "Just leave."

Dade's nerves were too close to the surface, too, and touching Kayla certainly hadn't helped. He felt ornerier than usual, and that wasn't good because he was the king of ornery. Best to go ahead and lay down some ground rules.

Dade aimed his index finger at Kenneth. "You draw that gun and I'll shoot you where you stand. Got that?"

Oh, the man wanted to argue all right. Dade could see it in his eyes, but he knew what was in his own eyes—determination to finish this damn job so he could get the heck out of there.

When Kenneth finally eased his hand away

from his weapon, Dade turned back to Kayla. "Where's your baby?"

She pulled back her shoulders. "That's none of your business."

He tapped his badge in case she'd forgotten. "This isn't personal, lady. I'm asking because I need to establish some security measures." He got closer, violating her personal space and then some.

Not the brightest idea he'd ever had. His chest brushed against her breasts, and he got a fire-hot reminder that Kayla was a woman.

Dade held his ground and met her eye-to-eye. "Where's your son?" he repeated.

She didn't back down, either. "He's sleeping upstairs. Now tell me what this is all about."

Dade ignored her question. "Is your son away from the windows?"

She stepped back and her breath rattled in her throat. "Why?"

Dade gave her a flat look. "Because my protective custody extends to your son, Robert."

"Robbie," she corrected, although she looked as if she wanted to curse for giving him even that little bit of personal information about her child. A kid who was supposedly just eleven months old. A baby. And it was because of the baby that Dade had quit arguing about this assignment so he could drive out to the Brennan estate.

He didn't care a rat's you-know-what about Kayla, but he would do everything within his power to protect an innocent child.

Even her child.

"The deputy's trying to scare you," Kenneth interjected.

"Yeah, I am," Dade readily admitted. He looked at her again to make sure she got what he was saying. "And if you have any sense whatsoever, you'll be scared because you can't believe Brennan is going to let you get anywhere near that witness stand tomorrow morning."

Her bottom lip trembled a little, but she kept her chin up and her expression resolute.

"Your baby's safety is one of the main reasons for the protective custody," Dade informed her. "I have to take your son and you to a safe house. Sheriff's orders."

She started the head shaking again. "I've already had someone upgrade the security system, and I can hire more bodyguards." Kayla looked at him. "I wouldn't have come back here to Silver Creek if I hadn't thought I could keep my son safe."

Dade made sure they had eye contact again. "You thought wrong."

She glanced out the sidelight window. "I don't believe that. Charles wouldn't do anything that would risk hurting Robbie."

"That's a chance you're willing to take?"

She didn't answer that. "Besides, I don't trust you any more than I trust Charles."

Dade couldn't blame her. The Rylands hadn't exactly been friendly since Ellie's murder. Things would stay that way, too, but it wouldn't stop Dade from doing his job.

Kayla stepped closer to him. So close that he caught her scent. Not perfume but baby powder.

"I'll call my attorney," she said with her voice lowered. "But I'm certain you can't force protective custody on me."

She was right. Well, unless he thought she was going to run. But because she'd arrived voluntarily, he didn't exactly have reason to believe she would leave.

"Think about your son's safety," Dade reminded her.

"I am." And she turned and opened the

door. "I can keep him safe without so-called help from the Rylands."

Fine. Dade had warned his brother and the D.A. that this wouldn't be an easy notion to sell, and both had told Dade that somehow he had to convince Kayla otherwise. Well, he'd failed, but he darn sure wasn't going to lose any sleep over it.

Dade was barely an inch out the door when Kayla slammed it so hard that he felt the gust of air wash over him. It mixed with the blast of chilly February wind that came right at him. He waited a second until he heard her engage the lock. He waited an extra second to see if she would change her mind, but when she didn't reopen the door, Dade cursed and headed off the porch and toward his truck.

Hell.

He really didn't want to go back to the sheriff's office and tell his brother, Grayson, that he'd failed. Not that Grayson was likely keeping count or anything, but Dade figured he already had too many failures on his records. Far more than the other deputies in Silver Creek. Still, he couldn't force a hard-headed woman to listen to reason.

Dade opened the door to his truck, moved

to get inside and then stopped. He lifted his head, listened and looked around.

The area surrounding the circular drive and front of the estate was well lit so he had a good view of pretty much everything within thirty yards in any direction. But it wasn't the lit areas that troubled him. It was the thick clusters of trees and shrubs on the east and west sides of the estate.

He waited, trying to tamp down the bad feeling he had about all of this. But the bad feeling stayed right with him, settling hard and cold in his stomach.

Dade cursed, shoved his truck keys in his pocket and headed back for the estate. He didn't relish going a second round with the curvy Kayla, but he would for the sake of her son. Dade turned. Made it just one step.

And that's when the shot rang out.

Chapter 2

Kayla was halfway up the stairs, but the sound stopped her cold.

A sharp, piercing blast.

The sound tore through the house. And her.

She froze for just a second, but Kenneth certainly didn't. He drew his gun.

"Get down!" Kenneth shouted. "Someone just fired a shot."

Kayla's heart started to pound, and her breath began to race. She had no intentions of getting down. She had to get to her baby. She had to protect Robbie.

There was another shot, followed by someone banging on the front door.

"Let me in!" that someone shouted. It was Deputy Dade Ryland. He was cursing, and while he bashed his fist against the door, he continued to yell for them to let him inside before he got killed.

Her first thought was that Dade was responsible for the shots, but that didn't make sense. He'd come here to warn her of danger, and if he'd wanted to shoot at them, then he could have done it in the foyer at point-blank range. Still, that didn't mean she trusted the deputy.

"You need to get down," Kenneth warned her again, and he headed to the door to disengage the security system and let in the deputy.

Dade didn't wait for the door to be fully open. The moment Kenneth cracked it, he dived through nearly knocking down her bodyguard in the process. The deputy had his gun drawn and ready, and he reached over to slap off the lights. In the same motion, he kicked the door shut.

"Lock it and reset the security system," Dade ordered Kenneth. He took out his phone from his jeans pocket and called for backup.

Even though he'd turned off the lights in the foyer, Kayla had no trouble seeing Dade because the lamp in the adjacent living room was blazing. Dade's eyes were blazing, too, and he turned that hot glare on her.

"I heard your bodyguard tell you to get down. What part of that didn't you understand?" Dade barked.

"I have to get to my son," she barked right back, and Kayla continued up the stairs. Or rather that's what she tried to do, but the third shot wasn't just a loud blast. It ripped through the window in the living room, spewing glass everywhere. And worse, the bullet tore into the stair railing just a few yards below her.

She froze. Oh, mercy. Someone wasn't just shooting. The person was actually trying to kill her.

"Now will you get down?" Dade demanded.

Without warning, Dade aimed his gun into the living room and fired, the blast echoing through the foyer. He shot out the lamp, plunging them into darkness. It took a moment for her eyes to adjust.

Even over the blast still roaring in her ears, Kayla heard a sound that robbed her of what little breath she had left. Robbie started to cry. He wasn't alone. The nanny, Connie Mullins, was with him, but Kayla didn't want to count on the petite sixty-year-old woman when it came to a situation like this.

A situation that had turned deadly.

Kayla refused to think of the possibility this could end with her death. And that wouldn't even be a worst-case scenario. Worst case would be for Robbie to get hurt.

Dade pointed to the living room where he'd just shot out the light. "Can you see the SOB shooting at your boss?" he asked Kenneth.

Her bodyguard shook his head, and both men glanced up at her as she started to crawl toward the nursery.

Dade cursed. "Cover me," he said to Kenneth. The order barely made it out of his mouth when he came barreling up the stairs, his cowboy boots hitting against the hardwood steps.

But that wasn't the only sound.

More shots came. One right behind the other. Each of them ripped through the expensive carved-wood railing and sent splinters flying in every direction. That didn't stop Dade. He made it to her, crawling over her to shove her as low as she could get.

"Robbie," she managed to say.

Dade's gaze slashed to hers. "If you go to him, the bullets will follow you."

That was the only possible thing he could have said to make her stop.

Kayla froze, and the full impact of that warning slammed into her as hard as the bullets battering the foyer. Oh, no. She'd put her son in danger. This was the very thing she'd tried to avoid, the very reason she'd come out of hiding, and she had only made it worse.

Again.

The anger collided with the fear, and she wanted to hit her fists against the stairs. She wanted to scream out for the shooter to stop. But more than those things, she just wanted to protect her baby.

"Is your son with a nanny?" Dade asked.

Kayla managed a nod. She'd asked Connie to wait in the nursery when she heard Dade ring the doorbell. "In there," she said, pointing to the first door off the left hall.

"Are they near a bathroom with a tub?" he also wanted to know.

Another nod. "There's one adjoining the nursery." And Kayla hated that she hadn't thought of that herself. "Connie?" she shouted.

"What's going on, Kayla?" the woman shouted back.

"I'm not sure," Kayla lied. "Just take Robbie into the bathroom and get in the tub." The porcelain tub would be their shield against the bullets.

Robbie was still crying, and the sound of her son's wails let her know that Connie was on the move. Robbie's voice became more and more faint until Kayla couldn't hear him at all.

That didn't help her nerves.

Hearing him had at least allowed her to know that he was all right. Still, she didn't want him out in the open in the nursery in case this attack continued.

As if to prove to her that it would, more bullets ripped through the foyer.

"How long before backup arrives?" Kenneth shouted.

"Too long," Dade answered. "At least fifteen minutes. This place isn't exactly in city limits."

Kenneth cursed and took cover behind a table. Kayla silently cursed as well. In fifteen minutes they could all be dead.

"I have to move you," Dade informed her. Other than a glance that had an I-told-you-this-could-happen snarl to it, his attention volleyed between the living room and the front door.

Kayla shook her head. "But you said I can't go near Robbie."

"You can't. But it's only a matter of time before the shooter changes positions." He tipped his head toward the front. "There are a lot of windows, and he'll have a clean shot once he moves."

Not *if* he moves but *once.*

"I'll roll to the side, just a little," Dade instructed. "And without standing up, I want you to get to the top of the stairs. Duck behind the first thing you see that can provide some cover."

Kayla managed to nod, and the moment that Dade lifted his weight off her, she did as he'd ordered. She covered her head with her hands and scrambled up the stairs as fast as she could.

The shots didn't stop, and one plowed into the wall above her just as Kayla dived to the side of a table. She'd barely managed that when Dade came barreling toward her. He hooked his arm around her waist and dragged her away from the table, away from the wall.

But also away from the nursery.

He hauled her toward the right, the opposite side from where Robbie and the nanny were, and Kayla was thankful that Dade had given her son that extra cushion of security. However, there was no cushion for Dade and her. They were off the stairs, yes, but the bullets continued to come at them. Dade flattened her on the floor and crawled back over her.

Kayla was well aware of his body pressed hard against hers. His breathing, too, because it was gusting in her ear. But she also felt his corded muscles and the determination to keep her alive.

That didn't mean, however, he'd succeed.

And that both frightened and infuriated her.

Just like that, the shots stopped. Kayla held her breath, waiting and praying that this was over, but it was Dade's profanity that let her know it wasn't.

She glanced back at him, and her gaze collided with those steel grays. He barely looked at her, but in that glimpse he managed to convey his concern and his disgust.

He hated her.

All the Rylands hated her. And Kayla couldn't blame them. Guilt by association. Her father-in-law had probably caused Ellie Ryland's death. And so far, he'd gotten off scot-free, thanks to a team of good lawyers and a technicality in some of the paperwork that had been used in his original arrest.

"What?" Dade snarled.

It took her a moment to realize he was talking to her, and she knew why. She was staring at him.

"Nothing," Kayla mumbled. And she forced her attention away from the one man who should disgust her as much as the shooter outside. But much to her dismay, what she felt wasn't total disgust.

Yet more proof that she was stupid.

She had noticed Dade Ryland's storm-black hair. It was a little too long, and his five o'clock stubble was a little too dark for her to think of him as handsome. No. It was worse than that. He wasn't handsome.

He was hot in that bad-boy, outlaw sort of way.

Well, she'd already been burned by one bad boy, and she wasn't looking for another. Not now. Not ever again.

Dade gave her another glance, and she could have sworn he smirked, as if he could read her mind.

"You see the shooter yet?" Dade called down to the bodyguard.

"No."

"The shooter's probably moving," Dade growled. He levered himself up just slightly and re-aimed his gun toward the front of the house.

Kayla could do nothing other than hope this would end with her baby unharmed. She'd been a fool to come back, a fool to respond to Charles's latest threat.

But what else could she have done?

She had to get out from beneath the hold Charles had on her. She had to try to make a safe, normal life for her son. But instead, she'd gotten this.

"Someone told Charles I was here," she mumbled. "Probably the D.A. or a Ryland." She hadn't meant to say Dade's family name so loudly, but by God it was hard to tamp down the anger while bracing for another attack.

"No one in my family is responsible for this," Dade informed her. "Lady, you got into this mess all by yourself."

She wanted to argue, but the sound stopped her. In the distance she heard sirens. No doubt the backup that Dade had called. Even though she didn't like the idea of the place crawling with any more Rylands, it was better than the alternative.

She hoped.

Beneath them in the foyer, Kayla heard her bodyguard moving around. Maybe so he could try to spot the shooter. Dade moved, too. He used his forearm to push her face back to the carpet, and he maneuvered himself off her. This time not just an inch or two. He reared up and took aim at the front windows.

He fired.

The blast roared through her ears, and she had no time to recover before there was another shot. Not from Dade. This one came tearing through the foyer but from a different angle than before. This bullet took out one of the front windows and sent glass flying through the air.

Dade had been right. The shooter had moved. And now Dade and she were in his direct line of fire.

For a few moments at the beginning of the attack, Kayla had hoped the shots were meant as a warning. A way to get her to grab Robbie and go back into hiding. But this was no warning.

This was an assassination attempt.

Dade sent another shot the gunman's way, and she put her hands over her ears to shut out the painful noise. However, she could still hear them. And the siren. It grew closer and closer as the gunman's shots came faster and faster. He wasn't panicking, and he definitely wasn't running. He was trying to kill her before the sheriff arrived.

"Stay down," Dade warned her. He shifted his gun toward one of the other front windows and fired.

This time, Kayla heard another sound. A groan of some kind, following by a heavy thud. Had Dade managed to shoot the gunman? Maybe.

Kayla looked up and followed the direction of Dade's aim. There. Through the jagged shards of glass jutting from the window frame, she saw something.

A man.

He was dressed head to toe in black, and it was only because of the porch light that she could see his silhouette. She could also see his gun, and he took aim at Dade and her.

Kayla yelled for Dade to get down, and she latched onto him to pull him back to the floor. But he threw off her grip and fired at the shadowy figure.

The man fired a shot as well and then clutched his shoulder. She couldn't be sure, but she thought this time maybe Dade had managed to shoot him.

Dade must have thought that too because he headed down the stairs, taking them two at a time while he kept his gun trained on the person on the porch. Kayla could only watch with her breath held and her heart pounding so hard that it might come out of her chest.

The man on the porch fired.

She yelled to warn Dade, but her warning was drowned out by another shot and the sounds of the approaching sirens. She heard Dade curse as if in pain, but what he didn't do was get down. He raced toward the door, threw it open and fired again.

But so did the gunman.

Oh, God.

She realized then that if this assassin managed to kill Dade that he would come after Robbie and her next. Of course, Kenneth was down there, somewhere, but if the gunman got past the bodyguard, then Kayla would have no way to defend her baby and herself.

Kayla cursed herself for not bringing some kind of weapon with her. But she wouldn't need a weapon if this goon tried to get to her baby. No. Pure raw adrenaline and the need to protect her child would give her the strength to fight whoever came through that door.

She stood, preparing herself for whatever she had to do, but instead she saw the blue swirls of the lights from a police cruiser. Red lights, too, maybe from an ambulance. The vehicles tore across the lawn and screamed to a halt. There were no more shots, just the noise of the men who scrambled from those vehicles.

Kayla waited, the seconds clicking off like gunshots in her head, and when the waiting became unbearable, she began to make her way down the stairs. The foyer was still dark, and the only illumination came from the jolts of red and blue lights from the responding vehicles.

"Kenneth?" she called out, her voice hardly more than a hoarse whisper. He didn't answer. "Deputy Ryland?" she tried.

No answer from Dade either.

Kayla inched down the steps, praying this ordeal was indeed over but also bracing herself for whatever she might see.

She didn't brace herself enough.

There was blood on the floor of the foyer.

In the darkness it looked like a pool of liquid black, but she instinctively knew what it was.

And there, slumped in the doorway was Dade Ryland.

Chapter 3

Dade looked down at his left arm and cursed. This was not a good time to get shot.

Hell.

Using the doorjamb for support, he got to his feet and tried not to look as if his arm was on fire. He figured he'd failed big-time when he saw Kayla. Her eyes were wide, her face way too pale.

"You've been shot," she said, the words rushing out.

Was that concern he saw and heard? He had to be wrong about that. No, this was probably just a reaction to the blood. And there was no doubt about it, there was blood.

"Check on your bodyguard," Dade barked, and he pulled back his shoulders so he could face the responders who were coming right at him.

First, there was his brother, Sheriff Grayson Ryland. Tall and lanky like most of his five siblings, Grayson might not have been the biggest of the half-dozen people who came out of the cruisers and ambulance, but he was automatically the center of attention and the one in charge. Grayson commanded respect just by stepping onto the scene.

Another brother, Mason, stepped out from a vehicle, too—a weathered Ford truck that had been red once, maybe twenty years ago. Mason, like Dade, was also a deputy sheriff but worked only part-time because he also ran the family ranch.

Dressed in his usual black jeans, black shirt and equally black Stetson, Mason made his way toward the estate. Not with Grayson's speed, authority or concern. Mason always looked as if he were stalking something. Or headed to a funeral.

"You're hurt," Grayson said, and he used his head to motion to the medics so they'd hurry to Dade. Grayson also kept his gun trained on the man sprawled out on the porch.

The dead man.

Dade had managed to take the guy out, but not before the SOB had fired a shot into Dade's arm. Talk about a rookie mistake, and he hadn't been a rookie in fourteen years, not since he'd joined the Silver Creek sheriff's department on his twenty-first birthday. Considering that being a cop was his one-and-only desire in life, he always seemed to be screwing it up.

Like now, for instance.

The gunman who could have given them answers was as dead as a doornail. Added to that, Dade had nearly let Kayla Brennan be gunned down, her bodyguard had been shot, or worse, and the jagged slice on his arm from the bullet graze was hurting like hell.

Grayson stooped down and put his fingers to the gunman's neck. "He's dead."

Yeah. No surprise there. "You need to check on Kayla's bodyguard," Dade let his brother know. He would do it himself, but he wanted a chance to catch his breath and get ahead of the pain.

"Kayla?" Grayson questioned, standing upright. He aimed a questioning glare at Dade, and Dade knew why. *Kayla* was way

too personal to call someone who might be responsible for a family member's death.

Grayson was right, and Dade silently cursed that, too. He was a sucker for a damsel in distress, and while he wasn't sure about the damsel part, Kayla was definitely in distress.

And so was her baby.

With his glare morphing into a disgusted scowl, Grayson flipped on the lights and walked past him and into the foyer where Kayla was kneeling down next to Kenneth.

"He's still breathing," Kayla announced, and that sent two of the medics scurrying in the bodyguard's direction.

One medic, however, Carrie Collins, a leggy brunette in snug green scrubs made a beeline toward Dade.

"I'm okay," Dade tried to tell her, but she latched onto his arm to examine it.

"I'll decide if you're okay or not," Carrie answered.

Like Kayla, there was way too much concern in her voice and expression. In this case, though, Dade knew why. Carrie and he had once been lovers, but that wasn't just water under the bridge. The water had dried up nearly a year ago. Too bad Carrie didn't always remember that.

"You need stitches," Carrie mumbled, her forehead bunching up. "And probably a tetanus shot."

But Dade tuned her out and put his attention on Kayla, Grayson and the unconscious bodyguard. Grayson caught onto Kayla and moved her away from the man so the medics could get to work, but it was obvious Kayla had tried to help her employee. Her hands and dress were covered with blood.

Kayla looked down at her palms, which were shaking almost violently, and she shuddered. Now that the lights were back on, Dade also saw the tears well up in her eyes.

Dade's feet seemed to have a mind of their own because he started toward her. So did Mason. Mason grunted and glanced down at Dade's arm.

"You scratched yourself," Mason remarked with zero sympathy in his tone. "Don't expect me to do the paperwork for this goat rope."

It was just what Dade needed to hear. Sarcasm without sympathy. He knew his brother loved him. Well, Dade was pretty sure of that anyway. But Mason wasn't the sort to cut anyone any slack.

Unlike Kayla. Blinking back tears, she

made her way toward Dade with her attention fixed on him. "I thought you'd been killed."

Dade was aware that both his brothers were watching and listening. "No. You didn't get lucky this time."

She flinched as if he'd slapped her, but quickly regained her composure. "Lucky?" she challenged. "Right. Well, let's just say I'm grateful you did your job and put yourself in front of bullets for me." Her voice trailed off to a whisper. "Thank you, Dade."

Dade was one-hundred-percent positive that his brother hadn't missed the way his given name had just purred right off her sympathetic rose-tinged lips. Or maybe the purring and the sympathy were his imagination.

Oh, man.

Kayla was going to be trouble with a capital *T.*

"I have to check on my baby," she let them know.

Dade snagged her by the arm. "Have the nanny and Robbie stay in the bathroom, okay? This might not be over."

As expected, the fear returned to her eyes. She swallowed hard, nodded and raced up the stairs.

"I'll need to question you when you come back down," Grayson called out to her.

Without looking back, she gave another shaky nod.

Dade wanted to hit himself in his fire-burning arm just to get his mind off this asinine need to comfort and to play nice with the one woman he shouldn't want to comfort or play nice with.

The three of them watched her make her way up the stairs, and Dade waited for the lecture from his brothers. A lecture that would no doubt include a reminder to think with his brain and not with what was behind the zipper of his Wranglers. But the lecture didn't come.

Not verbally anyway.

Grayson stepped away to give the medics some instructions, and then he took out his phone to call the county medical examiner, something Dade should have already thought to do.

"Did the dead guy give you any warning before he started shooting?" Mason asked.

Dade shook his head. "Kayla…" He considered calling her Ms. Brennan, but heck, the damage had already been done. "She refused protective custody, and I was on my way back to town when I figured out something was wrong. The guy opened fire before I could get back inside."

Mason stayed quiet a moment, but his forehead bunched up. "She refused our help." It wasn't a question. Mason sort of growled it out in a disapproving way.

Dade shrugged and then winced when that sent another shot of fire through his arm. "Understandable. She doesn't trust us. Just like we don't trust her."

Mason made a sound, one of his grunts that could have meant anything. Or nothing at all. "I'll keep watch outside. We don't need any more of Charles Brennan's henchmen showing up here tonight."

No, they didn't. And it could happen all right. Dade figured there was no way Brennan was going to let Kayla get anywhere near a witness stand.

"I need to clean that wound," Carrie let him know.

"Later." Dade moved to the side so the medics could take the bodyguard out on the gurney. Grayson had finished with his call and Dade wanted an update. Thankfully, Carrie didn't follow him.

"The M.E.'s on the way," Grayson relayed.

"And the rest of the deputies. Once they arrive, we can get *Kayla* and her baby out of here."

Dade glanced at the pool of blood and the shards of glass on the glossy marble floor. Maybe that would convince her to accept protective custody and leave for someplace safer.

If a safe place actually existed.

"Did she say why she changed her mind about testifying and came back to Silver Creek?" Grayson asked.

Dade shook his head and looked in the direction of the footsteps he heard. Kayla was making her way back downstairs, and she was no longer wearing the blood-soaked dress. She'd put on black pants and a gray blouse. She'd also adjusted her attitude. No more threat of tears or sympathetic looks. She was sporting a first-class glare.

"How's your son?" Dade asked, pleased that he would have to deal with the real Kayla rather than the damsel.

"He's fine," she snapped and then turned her attention to Grayson. "Someone obviously leaked my location," she accused before she even reached them in the foyer.

"Seems that way," Grayson admitted. "I suppose you think it was one of us."

"I do."

Dade stepped in front of his brother so he could finish this fight. "We have better things to do than endanger a witness. So that means the leak came from your side. Who knew you were coming here?"

She folded her arms over her chest. "You mean besides the Rylands?"

"Yeah, besides the *cops*." Dade didn't budge an inch. He met her eye-to-eye and practically foot-to-foot. But when she glanced down, Dade looked as well and saw the drop of his blood that had spattered onto one of her high-priced shoes.

"You need stitches," Grayson grumbled.

"I need answers from Ms. Brennan," Dade grumbled right back. But he did step slightly away so he wouldn't bleed on her fancy clothes.

And speaking of clothes, she'd missed a button on the blouse. Why he noticed that now, he didn't know.

Wait, yeah, he did know.

His male brain was too alert to the fact that Kayla was a woman. A woman with a gap in her blouse that allowed him a peek of the top of her right breast.

Dade did a double take.

She had a tattoo, a little pink heart right there on the swell of her breast.

Kayla made a soft sound of outrage, obviously noticing what had caught his attention, and she quickly buttoned her blouse as if she'd declared war on it.

"Your son's nanny knew you were here," Dade reminded her. He rolled up his shirt sleeve to put some pressure against his grazed arm.

She gave him a flat look. "My nanny is not responsible for this. She was in just as much danger as we were."

Dade couldn't argue with that. "So who else knew?"

Kayla wearily touched her fingers to her forehead. "My sister, Misty Wallace, but she wouldn't have told anyone."

Grayson and Dade exchanged glances, and Dade knew that Grayson would verify that as soon as he could.

Kayla noticed that glance and must have realized what it meant. "Don't waste your time with my sister. I trust her with my life, and she would die rather than tell Charles where I am. Instead, investigate the D.A.," she answered, her voice edged with anger.

"Winston Calhoun's not in the business of

killing witnesses, either," Dade let her know, although he would check to make sure the D.A. hadn't accidentally said the wrong thing to the wrong person. "I've known Winston my whole life. We can trust him."

"Maybe not," Kayla disagreed. "Is he rich like you and your family?"

"No." And Dade didn't like where this was going. "But not everyone can be bribed."

"My former father-in-law has a knack for finding a person's weak spot and getting his way." There was no smugness in her statement, and a frustrated sigh left her mouth.

He couldn't argue with that, either. "What about your sister, then? Is Misty dirty rich like you?"

Oh, that got a rise out of her. The anger flashed through her eyes. "This isn't about Misty. It's about Charles and whomever he could have bribed."

"Maybe," Dade concluded. "Then I'll go back to my original question. Who knew you were coming here? A boyfriend? A lover?"

She shook her head and looked ready to slug him. "No, on both counts."

"Your driver, then." Dade tried again.

"I drove myself, and I didn't tell anyone else where I was going." She paused. She glanced around the foyer, her attention landing on Dade's bloody arm. "I came here because I thought Charles would believe this was the last place I'd be."

"Obviously you got that wrong," Dade grumbled.

"Obviously," she grumbled right back.

"Why did you change your mind about testifying?" Dade pressed when she added nothing else.

Kayla dodged his gaze. "You wouldn't believe me if I told you."

Because she was staring at the floor, Dade ducked down a little to make eye contact. "Try."

She lifted her shoulder, stepped away from him. "I wanted to do the right thing." Kayla paused. "This morning, I got a threatening email from my ex-father-in-law."

Dade and Grayson exchanged another glance. "You told the D.A. about this?" Grayson asked.

"No, what would have been the point? Charles's threats are nothing new and never specific enough to bring charges against him. But this time, something inside me… snapped." She paused. "Or maybe for the first time things got crystal clear." Her gaze came to Dade's again, and she blinked back tears. "After reading that email, I knew the only way I could get this to stop was to testify and make sure Charles is put away for the rest of his life."

Oh, hell. There it was again. Sympathy. It was burning as hot as the gash on his arm. Grayson obviously wasn't immune either because he gave a heavy sigh.

"And that's the reason I need you in protective custody," Grayson concluded. "I want to take you and your baby to a safe house so that Brennan can't get to either of you. Brennan is out of jail on bond, and we're trying to keep an eye on him. But you know better than anyone, he can hire guns to do his dirty work."

Kayla stared at Grayson. Then stared at Dade, too. "After what happened tonight, how can you possibly keep my baby safe?" she asked. Her voice broke on the last word.

Dade was about to assure her that he would do his best, but Grayson's phone rang. He glanced at the screen and mumbled some profanity before he stepped away to take the call.

"I still don't trust you," Kayla whispered to Dade.

He nodded. "Yeah, I get that." He pointed to the blood on the floor. "But you've got a very short list of people you can trust right now."

She must have known that was true, but she still didn't agree.

"That was one of the medics," Grayson relayed, putting his phone back in his pocket. He walked back across the foyer toward them, his attention nailed to Kayla. "Your bodyguard died on the way to the hospital."

That was all he said. Grayson didn't offer any details or reiterate that she could have been the one in that ambulance.

Kayla pulled in her breath, and what little color she had drained from her face. She gave one crisp nod and turned toward the stairs. "I'll let the nanny know that we're moving to a safe house tonight with Dade—Deputy Ryland," she corrected, her voice now chilled with that ice-queen tone.

Dade didn't exactly celebrate because it had taken way too long to convince her to do the right thing. Now, he only hoped it *was* the right thing. After all, she'd just put her son's and her lives right in his hands.

"I think we might have found our leak," Mason said, stepping into the doorway.

That got everyone's attention. Kayla

stopped on the bottom step and turned to face him.

"I checked the dead gunman's phone." Mason held up the bagged cell for them to see. "About a half hour before this guy started shooting, he made three calls." He aimed his usual surly expression at Kayla. "First one was to some guy named Danny Flynn, a low-life who likely works for your ex-father-in-law, Charles Brennan."

"He does," Kayla admitted. "I remember that name."

Well, that wasn't exactly a bombshell. Everyone knew how much Brennan wanted to stop Kayla. Of course, Brennan would deny any association with the employee who'd gotten the call, but the cops might be able to break the employee and get him to confess.

"You said you'd found the leak?" Dade prompted.

Mason glanced at the screen on the dead man's cell. "We got two possibilities. The next call the gunman made was to Misty Wallace."

The breath seemed to swoosh right out of Kayla. "My sister?"

"Your sister," Mason confirmed.

Kayla frantically shook her head. "But

Misty wouldn't tell Charles or anyone else where I was going."

"Right," Mason grumbled. "That call to her says otherwise." He went to Grayson and handed him the phone so that his brother could also check out the screen.

From his angle Dade couldn't see what caused both his brothers' eyes to narrow.

Kayla had a white-knuckled grip on the stair railing. "Who's the third person he called?"

"What kind of game are you playing, Ms. Brennan?" Grayson demanded.

"What do you mean?" And her shock sure as heck sounded sincere.

But Dade didn't take her sincerity of the head shaking at face value. He leaned in so he could see the name of the last person the gunman had called.

Hell.

What was going on?

Chapter 4

Kayla was trembling, but that didn't stop her from marching across the foyer to see what had caused the Rylands to turn those accusing stares on her. And then she saw the cell phone screen.

No, it couldn't be. But it was.

It was her name and number.

"Why did the gunman call you?" Dade demanded.

"He didn't," Kayla answered as quickly as she could get out the words.

"The phone says otherwise," Mason Ryland growled.

"Then it was faked somehow." She hated

the quiver in her voice. Hated even more that she cared one iota what these Rylands thought of her, but by God she'd had no part in this attack. "I wouldn't have hired someone to shoot into a house where my son was staying."

The trio exchanged glances. A united brotherly front against her. They didn't just look alike—they had the same scowls. And they were also waiting for more of an explanation. However, Kayla didn't have one.

"Where's your phone?" Dade asked after first giving an impatient huff.

She glanced around but didn't see it and remembered she hadn't seen it upstairs, either. Just moments before Dade's arrival, she'd been searching through her purse for it. "I must have left it in my car." She pointed to the side of the estate where she'd parked.

Even though none of the lawmen came right out and accused her of lying, it was clear from their deepening scowls they didn't believe her.

"I'll look for it," Mason insisted, and he strolled out, leaving her to face the remaining two.

"I didn't speak to the gunman," Kayla tried again. "And if he called me, it was to set me up."

"Why would he do that?" Grayson asked.

Kayla didn't have to think too hard to come up with an answer. "Maybe to try to discredit my testimony. Charles could have hired the gunman to do that because if he could prove I had an association with a killer, then it might make a jury less likely to believe anything I say."

Another exchange of glances before Grayson spoke again. "Or *you* could have hired the gunman to make Brennan look guilty of attempted murder. A crime that could put him away for life and not just the twenty years he'd get for the other charges."

Oh, mercy. As theories went, it wasn't a bad one, and Kayla had no idea how she would convince the Rylands that she was innocent.

"Maybe your sister is the one who did the hiring." Dade tossed that out there, not tentatively, but it wasn't a roaring declaration of Kayla's innocence, either.

But what had she expected?

Yes, Dade had saved her life. Had even been wounded in the process, but to him she was lower than dirt. Well, except for those heated looks that he hadn't quite been able to suppress. Kayla was too familiar with those looks. Her late-husband, Preston, had certainly given her enough of them, and she was painfully aware of where that had gotten her.

"I'll call my sister," Kayla mumbled and started for the house phone that was on a table in the foyer. Of course, to get to it, she would literally have to walk through her dead bodyguard's blood.

"Here," Dade offered, handing her his cell.

Kayla took it, her hand brushing against his. Not a gentle hand, either. It was rough. No doubt from the physical labor of ranch work.

The adrenaline was playing havoc with her body and memory so it took her a while to remember Misty's number. She began to press it in when she heard Robbie. Not crying, but he was making fussy sounds, and those sounds were getting closer. Kayla looked at the stairs and saw her nanny, Connie, making her way toward them. The petite brunette looked completely weighed down with Robbie in the crook of her left arm and a suitcase gripped in her right hand.

Kayla stopped the call so she could go help, but Dade motioned for her to finish it. Instead, he hurried to the stairs, took the suitcase himself and set it on the floor. Robbie was rubbing his eyes and fussing when his attention landed on Dade. The fussing stopped, and much to Kayla's surprise, her son mumbled something indistinguishable and reached for the lawman.

Her surprise grew to shock when Dade reached out as well and eased Robbie into his arm.

"I have two other suitcases upstairs," Connie let him know, and she looked at Kayla. The nanny's eyebrow lifted to verify if it was all right for Dade to have hold of her son.

It wasn't all right, and Kayla moved to do something about that.

Just as her call to Misty went straight to voice mail.

"I'll get the suitcases," Grayson offered. "Show me where they are," he directed to Connie, and the two started up the stairs.

"Misty," Kayla said when the voice mail instructed her to leave a message, "call me immediately. I have to talk to you. It's important. I need to know if you told anyone where I'd be staying."

And with that done, Kayla hurried to Dade and practically wrenched Robbie away from him. That didn't make her son or Dade happy. The baby immediately started to cry, and

Dade winced when she bumped against his wounded arm.

"Sorry," she mumbled. Kayla eased Robbie's head against her shoulder and began to rock.

Dade gave her a flat look after he was done wincing. "I wasn't going to kidnap him."

"I know. It's just…" But she had no idea how to finish that explanation. At this point it would sound petty if she admitted that she didn't want her son in a Ryland's arms. "Misty didn't answer her phone, so I left a message."

Dade waited a moment, his stare drilling through her, and she earned another of those impatient huffs. "You do realize I'll be around the baby and you while you're in my protective custody?"

Kayla was sure she blinked. "But you're injured. I thought someone else would guard us." Preferably someone who wasn't a Ryland.

"No…." He stretched out the word. "This isn't an injury. It's a scratch, and it won't affect my aim if I need to take out another gunman."

Another gunman. That sent an icy chill through her. Thankfully, it was a chill her son didn't seem to notice because he finally calmed down and started to go back to sleep. But Kayla knew there would be no sleep for her in the immediate future.

And she knew who to thank for that.

"I need to make another call," she told Dade, and she didn't wait for his permission to use his cell. Nor did she have to try to remember this particular number. She'd seen it countless times on her own phone.

Charles Brennan answered on the first ring.

"Dade Ryland?" Charles greeted, though he sounded more amused than concerned. "Why would the deputy sheriff be calling?"

"No, Charles. It's me," Kayla informed him.

Dade rolled his eyes and reached for the phone, but she moved away from him and held on tight to both Robbie and Dade's cell.

"Did you send someone to kill me tonight?" she demanded from Charles.

"I don't know what you mean."

She listened for any differences in his voice. Anything that would confirm that he was behind this attack. But he sounded like his normal arrogant self.

"Someone hired a gunman to come after me," Kayla clarified, even though she was certain he already knew what she meant.

"And where are you exactly?" Charles asked. Still no change in his inflection.

Even though she doubted Dade had actually heard Charles's question, he got right in her face, and his scowl intensified. Something she hadn't thought possible.

"I'm at a place where I won't be much longer," Kayla answered. "And I want you to stop this now. Robbie could have been killed tonight."

"What?" Charles barked, and it had a cold, dangerous undercurrent to it.

"You heard me. The idiot you hired could have killed us all. Call off your dogs, Charles, and take your punishment like a man."

"I wouldn't have sent an idiot after you." And there was the change of inflective. It sounded as if he were telling the truth.

Sounded.

But Kayla had learned the hard way that Charles was capable of deception in its purest form. He certainly hadn't denied that he'd hired a hitman.

"The gunman phoned one of your goons," Kayla informed him, even though Dade gave her a have-you-lost-your-mind look. "I want you to call whomever it takes to make this stop."

Charles didn't answer right away. "I'll get back to you." And he hung up.

Dade threw up his hands and winced again. "Did it occur to you to ask me before you made a call to our number-one suspect?"

"I thought I was your number-one suspect," she snarled and thrust his phone at him.

He opened his mouth, probably to confirm that she was, but he didn't. Dade just shook his head, snatched his phone from her hand and stuffed it into the front pocket of his jeans. "That call accomplished nothing."

"Well, it made me feel better," Kayla fired back. It didn't. Nothing would make that happen, not with her bodyguard dead and the body of a hired assassin on her front porch.

Dade mumbled some profanity. "Don't do anything else that might end up helping your father-in-law, understand?"

Oh, that stung. She would never help Charles. *Never.* "Look, I know you don't believe me, but we're on the same page when it comes to my late-husband's father. It's possible Charles was responsible for your sister-in-law's death. Likely, even. But you couldn't possibly want him in jail more than I do."

Dade met her eye-to-eye. "Wanna bet?"

Kayla didn't dodge him. She held her

ground. "As long as Charles is free, I'm not. And neither is my son." Because she needed it, she brushed a kiss on Robbie's forehead. "It's not my fault that Charles isn't behind bars. If you want someone to blame, blame the cops who investigated Ellie Ryland's murder."

Dade didn't flinch, but it was close. Probably because his brother had been in on the investigation. Heck, all the Rylands had, even though it hadn't been their jurisdiction. In fact, the case had gone to the FBI when the lead investigator had uncovered some evidence of Charles's money laundering that was linked to a federal case.

"The FBI's search warrant was screwed up. It didn't include the storage facility at his estate," Dade reminded her. "And that meant all those files and records that were seized there couldn't be used to convict Brennan. To add insult to injury, there was no more proof to arrest him, much less get a conviction."

Kayla knew all of this by heart because she'd read the reports too many times to count. "Then blame the FBI. Blame Charles's team of lawyers who challenged the warrant in the first place. But know this—if I get the chance to put Charles away, I'm taking it. Not for you. Not for your late sister-in-law. But for my son. When are you going to believe me?"

The fit of temper and energy went as fast as it came, and Kayla felt beyond drained. Maybe that's why she hadn't heard Mason come back into the house. And he wasn't the only one to reappear. Grayson was at the top of the stairs, a suitcase in each hand, and all of them were staring at her again.

"Maybe we'll believe you when there's proof that you're innocent." That came from Mason—the dark and dangerous Ryland. The one who made her more nervous than even Dade. "Your phone wasn't in the car. I searched every inch of it."

Kayla wearily shook her head. "Then I must have lost it or left it at the condo where I was staying."

"Convenient," Mason mumbled.

"No, it's not," she argued, knowing it wouldn't do any good. "I wish I could produce the phone so you'd know I had no part in this."

"Call her cell," Grayson said, making his way down the stairs. "The number is there on the dead gunman's phone."

Kayla huffed and was about to tell any Ryland who would listen that calling her on the missing phone would be useless. She didn't have it with her in the house, and she honestly had no idea where it was. But she decided just to let them have their way.

Mason lifted the gunman's phone so he could see the numbers through the plastic bag, and he used his own cell to make the call.

Kayla's heart nearly stopped.

Because the moment that Mason finished pressing in the numbers, the sound shot through the foyer.

While the rest of them watched and while Kayla held her breath, Mason followed the sound.

He didn't have to go far.

Just a few feet away from her.

There, under the foyer table, at the edge of the pool of blood, her missing cell phone was ringing.

Chapter 5

Dade listened to Grayson's latest request and silently cursed.

Yeah.

This was going to be fun.

He snapped his phone shut, dropped it on the console between Kayla and himself and continued the drive to the safe house.

"We need your fingerprints so we can compare them to those on the cell we found in your foyer," Dade relayed to her. He whispered so he wouldn't wake Robbie.

Both the baby and the nanny, Connie, were asleep in the back seat of the SUV, and Dade wanted it to stay that way. They were less than ten minutes from the safe house, both clearly exhausted, and he'd have to wake them soon enough.

When Kayla didn't answer, Dade glanced at her. She was leaning against the window, her attention fastened to the side mirror. No doubt looking for another gunman who might try to follow them. Dade had done the same thing since he'd started the half-hour drive from her estate to the old Wellman ranch and had thankfully seen nothing but a coyote and a deer on the narrow country road.

"Fingerprints," she mumbled. "I have a juvenile record. You can probably get them from that."

"A juvenile record?" Dade hadn't meant to sound shocked, but he was.

"I was fifteen and stupid. I went for a joy-ride with a boy and didn't know he was driving a stolen car. When the cops stopped us, he told them we stole the car together."

All right. He had to think about that a moment. "I'm surprised a rich girl like you couldn't hire a good lawyer and get the charges thrown out." Dade hadn't meant it to sound so callous, but he had seen it happen too many times.

She gave him a look that could have frozen hell. "You know nothing about me. *Nothing*."

That was true. Until tonight Kayla had been the woman married to the mob. The daughter-in-law of a slimeball killer. And now she was Dade's responsibility.

Among other things.

She was also a woman, and he kept noticing that. Like now, for instance. Even though she was giving him that hell-freezing look, he could also see the fear and the weariness. Oh, and her hot body. He didn't want to think for one minute that it played into this, but he was afraid it did.

So did that little baby sleeping in the car seat behind him.

Dade might have been a bad boy with a badass reputation, but that kid had nearly turned him to mush when he'd reached for Dade in the foyer. The kid had something his mom didn't—complete trust that Dade would take care of him.

"My fingerprints will be on the phone," she reminded him. "Because it belongs to me."

"Yeah, but Kenneth's shouldn't be on it. Should they?"

"No." She paused a moment. "I'd been looking for my cell right before you arrived, and I'd just asked Kenneth if he'd seen it. He said no."

Well, that was a start. "So, if his prints are on it, then it could mean he was in on the attack."

Kayla shook her head before he even finished. "That doesn't make sense, either. If the gunman had called my cell and Kenneth had the phone on him, I think I would have heard it."

"Maybe it rang when you were upstairs with your son." And maybe Kenneth hadn't wanted her to hear it because he wanted to set Kayla up, to make her look guilty.

She shook her head. "If Kenneth and the gunman were both working for Charles, then why didn't Kenneth just kill me before you arrived? He had plenty of chances. And then why would the gunman have killed a fellow hired gun?"

Dade didn't have answers to her questions, but he hoped to remedy that soon. His laptop was in his bag, and he intended to spend most of the night working.

"The dead gunman's name is Raymond Salvetti," Dade told her. "Ring any bells?"

She sat up straighter in the seat and repeated it several times. "No. He has a record?"

"Oh, yeah. That's why Grayson was able to make such a quick ID."

Kayla blew out a long breath. "Did you connect him to Charles?"

"Not yet."

And maybe never.

Because Brennan would have known there was potential for the hired gun to be caught, he could have hidden the paper trail that would connect him to a possible killer. Still, that didn't mean they couldn't link Brennan to the dead bodyguard or to Danny Flynn, the other man the gunman had phoned. Flynn hadn't been at his residence when SAPD had checked, but his name and picture had been sent out to law-enforcement agencies throughout the state. Plus, Kayla could recognize the moron if he showed up.

Dade took the final turn down the ranch road and drove the last quarter of a mile to the house. He watched Kayla as she took in the place. It didn't take her long because there wasn't much to see—a simple wood frame house and two barns surrounded by acres of pasture and trees. There was no livestock, no other people, and there hadn't been since Pete

Wellman died three years earlier. He'd had no heirs, so Grayson had bought the place as an investment.

"Wait here a second," Dade ordered. He brought the SUV to a stop directly in front of the porch and the front door. Mason had already been out to put things in order, but Dade wanted to be sure.

He got out, went to the front door and unlocked it. Dade was pleased to hear the security alarm kick on. He disarmed it temporarily and did a walk-through. A living-dining combination. A kitchen. Three bedrooms. Two baths.

Tight quarters.

Especially because Kayla had a unique way of reminding him that she was around.

When Dade was satisfied that the house was indeed safe, he went back to the SUV to grab the suitcases. There were five total, and by the time he'd gotten them all inside and in place, a drowsy-looking Connie had already taken Robbie to the room that Kayla and the baby would share. Dade's room was in the middle. Not by accident either. He wanted to be able to hear if anything went wrong.

Once they were all inside, Dade didn't waste any time resetting the security system.

He was certain they hadn't been followed, but he didn't want any surprise visitors in the middle of the night. Just in case, he left on his shoulder holster and gun.

"Does the bandage on your arm need to be checked?" Kayla asked.

Dade was in the process of removing his jacket. And wincing. That's probably what had prompted her question. "No, it's fine."

He'd slathered the wound with antibiotic cream and bandaged it at the sheriff's office when they'd stopped to pick up the SUV and other equipment.

Kayla stared at him as if she might challenge him and then fluttered her fingers toward the bathroom. "I need to take a shower." And with that, she walked away.

Dade watched her.

In fact, he couldn't make himself look away. Well, until she glanced over her shoulder at him. Then, his attention flew to the bag he'd put next to the sofa. Time to get his mind on the investigation and off Kayla's backside. But man, the woman had some curves.

Dade grabbed a soda from the fridge that Mason had stocked, took out his laptop and sank onto the sofa. There were already emails and reports about the shooting. Of course, with two dead bodies there would be a lot more to follow.

He fired off an email to Grayson to let him know about Kayla's juvenile record and the possibility of getting fingerprints from that. Grayson answered almost immediately with a thanks.

Dade scanned through the rest of the reports until he got to an attachment with Kayla's name. It was the file with everything Grayson and the San Antonio police had gathered on her. Because Kayla and he would be joined at the hip for the next few days, Dade opened it so he could find out more about this woman who had his body zinging.

Kayla Wallace Brennan was thirty-one, four years younger than him. Born in Houston. Parents divorced when she was a kid. One sister, Misty. Kayla married Preston Brennan when she was barely twenty-four, and their marriage had lasted nearly six years. Six years was a long time to be under the influence of a mob family. A woman could pick up all kinds of nasty habits.

Dade scrolled down.

And his fingers froze on the keys.

There were pictures of Kayla. Not the cool, rich ice queen with a great butt. They were police photos taken three years ago. Her hair had been pulled back, no makeup, and the camera had gobbled up a dozen or more images of the bruises on her face and upper body. Her right eye was practically swollen shut. Her bottom lip, busted open.

Dade got a rock-hard knot in his stomach.

He skimmed through the report that followed the pictures, and that knot in his stomach tightened. Kayla hadn't been mugged. According to the report, her husband, Preston, had done this to her during a domestic dispute.

A day later, Kayla dropped the charges.

Hell's bells.

Dade had seen that happen before, but he hadn't thought this had gone on with Kayla.

That stomach knot quickly turned to raw anger. Preston had been a big guy, muscles on top of muscles, and he'd used his wife for a punching bag. Dade cursed some more and then nearly jumped out of his skin when he heard the sound.

A loud thump.

He came off the sofa, drew his gun and hurried in the direction of the sound. Dade braced himself to come face-to-face with a gunman or maybe even Charles Brennan.

But it was a naked Kayla against the wall.

Okay, she wasn't naked exactly. She had on a silky white bathrobe that had shimmied off her shoulder all the way to the top of her breast, and it was that naked part of her that grabbed his attention more than the clothed parts.

"I slipped," she mumbled and quickly righted the bathrobe. No more peeks at her breast and that tattoo. "My legs are like jelly."

Dade understood that. He suddenly felt a little wobbly, too. And aroused. Something he quickly pushed aside. But he did reholster his gun and catch onto her arm to steady her.

"It's the adrenaline crash," he let her know. "You should probably try to sleep it off."

She nodded, raked her hair from her face. "I just need a drink of water first."

Kayla eased out of his grip and stepped around him. At least she tried. But the hall was narrow, and they brushed against each other despite their efforts to avoid one another. Heck, she might as well have kissed him because that's the punch he felt in his body.

Dade put some distance between them and followed her. Best to get back to work. But he didn't succeed with that either because Kayla suddenly froze, her attention knifing right to the photos on his computer screen.

She made a sound, something small and helpless that came deep from within her throat. It was a split-second response before she steeled up again.

"Why are you looking at those?" she asked, but her voice wasn't nearly as steely as she was trying to appear to be.

"I was going through your files." And Dade left it at that. It seemed a sick violation of her privacy, but those pictures told him more about Kayla than he'd ever wanted to know.

She swallowed hard and went to the fridge to get a bottle of water. She gulped some down as if her throat were parched. "Preston had a mean streak," she mumbled.

Yeah. And even though it was stupid, Dade wished the mean-streaked moron was still around so he could beat him to a pulp. "So why did you stay with him?" Dade asked before he could stop himself.

Her forehead bunched up, and the corner of her mouth lifted. A dry half smile. "What you really want to know is why I let him do that to me." She drew in her breath. "Because at first I loved him. I thought he would change. And then I began to believe I deserved to be hurt."

Even though it pulled at his arm wound, Dade put his hands on his hips. "You thought you deserved *that?*" He didn't wait for her to answer. "Because you didn't. No woman deserves it."

She nodded. Hesitated and then nodded again. "I figured that out eventually and was in the process of filing for a divorce when he was killed in the car accident."

Again, Dade had to adjust everything he knew about this woman. Here she'd been a battered wife, pregnant, and yet she'd planned to divorce a man who would have likely tried to kill her.

"I'm sorry he did that to you. Real sorry," Dade mumbled.

She tried to shrug and then blinked hard. The tears were right there, threatening to spill. He debated if he should do anything, but his feet started toward her before the debate even had a chance.

Kayla whispered a soft "no" when Dade reached out. But she didn't step back, and that made it easy for him to ease his good arm around her and inch her to him. She went board stiff but still didn't move to stop him.

"This isn't a good idea," she reminded him, even though she was sniffing back tears.

"Yeah. I don't always lean toward the *good idea* approach. I'm more of a go-with-your-gut kind of guy." And with that, he pulled her to him.

"I don't want your sympathy," Kayla insisted, still sniffing.

"Okay, because I'm also not good with that. This is just a little human kindness, that's all. You've been to hell and back, and I'm guessing that started a long time before today. Before those pictures were taken."

"That sounds like sympathy to me," she complained.

Dade didn't argue and he didn't let go of her. "Then we'll strike a deal. We can still dislike each other. Heck, it can border on hate. I won't give you any sympathy, but we'll call a truce."

She made a sound of disagreement and eased back so they made eye contact. "A truce that involves hugs." Now, she stepped back, but that didn't seem to make her any happier. "I'm very vulnerable right now. I'm scared, and I have a horrible knack for allying myself with the worst person possible."

Dade cocked his head to the side. "You talking about Preston now or me?"

She froze a moment. "You. Preston can't hurt me anymore, but you, well, you can."

And he instinctively knew she wasn't talking about physical violence. He had never hit a woman, and if he got his hands on Kayla, the last thing he'd want to do is hit her.

"*I* would be a mistake," he said, but he didn't say it under his breath as he'd intended. It was plenty loud enough for her to hear.

The corner of her mouth lifted just a fraction and then lowered just as quickly. "The worst kind."

Yeah. He was in trouble the size of Texas here. Because now they weren't indirectly talking about something beyond truces and protective custody. They were talking about this damn attraction.

And sex.

Dade cursed. "I wish to hell I hadn't seen your tattoo."

Or those pictures on the computer. And while he was at it, he wished her scent would stop sliding through him. She smelled like a fairy princess, all flowery and soft.

A smile barely touched her lips. "The tattoo is a relic from my youth. And I wish you hadn't seen it, either."

That was what she was saying, but her

eyes were warm now. Not that riled spicy blue. This was more like the color of the sky. Calmer. Welcoming.

She opened her mouth, closed it and then motioned toward the hall. "Good night, Dade."

He didn't argue. He'd already said enough stupid things, and if she stayed, there would only be a greater opportunity for more stupidity. However, she only made it one step before Dade's phone buzzed.

"It's Grayson," he said, glancing at the screen. Dade answered it and hoped like the devil this call was good news. Any good news would do.

"Thanks for the email about Mrs. Brennan's juvenile record," Grayson started. "Her prints were there, and we were able to do a quick comparison. It's her prints on the cell, and the account is in her name."

It was exactly as they'd expected, and it certainly didn't make her guilty of anything other than owning a cell phone. "Any other prints?" Dade didn't exactly pray that there would be, but he considered it.

"Just smudges," Grayson let him know. "Nothing we can match."

Damn. Not good news because the phone

was pretty much a dead end. If Kenneth had indeed had the cell when the gunman called, then that was a secret that Kenneth had taken to his grave.

Dade locked eyes with Kayla who was hanging on to his every word. "What about the dead gunman's cell? Anything on it that'll help?" he asked Grayson.

"No breaks there. We're still looking for Danny Flynn. But we did locate the other person the gunman called."

"Misty Wallace?" Dade questioned, and that drew Kayla's full attention. She walked closer, and Dade went ahead and put the call on speaker.

"Yeah. San Antonio PD picked Misty up about twenty minutes ago," Grayson let Dade know.

SAPD. That meant his twin, Nate, had likely been involved in that pickup. Dade hated that Nate had to be part of this, but of course, he would be. Brennan was possibly the man who'd murdered Nate's wife. There was no way his brother would step back from this investigation.

"Nate will bring Misty here tomorrow morning so we can question her," Grayson added.

Kayla's fingers were trembling when she touched them to her mouth.

"Is Misty talking?" Dade immediately asked.

"Not to SAPD, but she says she'll talk to us. And she has a message for her sister. Misty wants you to tell her that she's sorry."

"Sorry about what?" Kayla said under her breath. It wasn't very loud but apparently loud enough for Grayson to hear.

Grayson grumbled something under his breath, too. "She wouldn't say, but I intend to find out."

Chapter 6

Kayla heard the sound, and her eyes flew open. It wasn't the sounds of bullets like those in her nightmares. This was laughter. And it was coming from the other side of the house.

"Robbie?" she called out and then remembered Connie had come and gotten him when he woke up earlier. The nanny had told Kayla to get a little more rest, and apparently she had.

She threw back the covers and spotted the sunlight speckling across the room from the tiny gaps in the blinds. She checked the clock on the nightstand—already seven-thirty. Not late by many people's standards, but she'd overslept.

How the heck could that have happened?

Here they were in the middle of a dangerous situation, and she'd slept in like the diva Dade already thought she was.

Kayla changed out of her gown and put on the dark blue pants and top that she practically ripped from her suitcase. She used the hall bathroom to finish dressing and raced toward the laughter. She soon found the source.

Her son.

Dade was at the kitchen table, Robbie in his lap, and her son was giggling because Dade was playing airplane with the spoon of oatmeal. Her son devoured the oatmeal the moment it made it to his mouth.

Kayla made eye contact with Connie who was near the stove pouring herself a cup of coffee. The nanny, who looked as if she had also dressed in a hurry, simply shrugged.

"Mommy's up," Dade announced, and he sent another spoonful of oatmeal Robbie's way. Another giggle. And her son lapped it up.

"I'm sorry," Kayla told Dade. "I should have been up to feed him."

Dade just shrugged as well. "I have a niece,

Kimmie, who's just a little bit older than Robbie, and I feed her a lot of mornings."

So that explained why the bad-boy cowboy looked perfectly natural with flecks of oatmeal on his jeans and chest-hugging black T-shirt. Robbie hadn't escaped, either. He had oatmeal smeared into his blond hair.

"I can take over," Kayla insisted. But when she looked in the bowl, she realized that Robbie had finished.

"Da-da-da," Robbie babbled, and he slapped his hands on the highchair tray.

Kayla was mortified and was about to launch into an apology for that, as well.

"He's trying to say Dade," Connie quickly explained.

Dade lifted his shoulder again. "That seems a little easier to say than Deputy Ryland."

Maybe, but it was downright unnerving to hear those sounds come from her son's mouth. More unnerving to see the big grin that Robbie doled out to Dade.

"Let me get him washed up," Connie insisted.

"I can do it," Kayla offered.

But Connie glanced at Dade. "I think the deputy and you have some things to discuss."

Yes, they did. Misty, for one, because her

sister had been brought in for questioning and had issued that vague *I'm sorry.* Kayla had tried to call her sister more than a dozen times before she went to bed, but Misty hadn't answered.

Connie eased Robbie out of the highchair and brought him over to Kayla so she could get a morning kiss. She got one all right, complete with oatmeal smears and a smile that could have lit up the night. Kayla had no choice but to smile back.

"I love you," she whispered to her son, and Robbie babbled back a string of sounds that could have meant anything. But Kayla knew he was telling her that he loved her, too.

"He's a fun kid," Dade said, and he got to his feet.

"Yes, but he's usually shy around strangers." Probably because Robbie hadn't been exposed to many, but he'd taken to Dade as if he'd known him his whole life.

Dade looked at her, as if waiting for more, but she didn't want to talk about how good he was with her son. Kayla also didn't want to stare. She failed at that. She stared. And wondered how anyone could look that good with flecks of oatmeal on them.

She reached up and plucked a piece of it from Dade's hair. "Robbie's a messy eater."

"Not as bad as Kimmie. Once she crammed a handful of strained peaches in my ear. Couldn't hear for hours." With that, he smiled.

Oh, mercy.

He was hot with his usual bad-boy scowl, but that smile made her weak at the knees. Kayla stepped back, cleared her throat and changed the subject. "When will Grayson question Misty?"

Dade's smile faded as fast as it'd come, and he checked the wall clock over the table. "Soon. They're setting up things now so we can watch. My laptop is already on, and I've connected to Grayson's computer at his office."

She glanced at his computer screen to verify that it was indeed on, and there on the screen was what appeared to be an office. An empty one.

"Watch?" she challenged. "But I thought I'd be able to see Misty in person."

"Not a chance," Dade informed her. "We aren't leaving this safe house unless it's an emergency."

Of course. That made sense for security

reasons. But Kayla had wanted to see her sister and not through a computer screen.

"We'll be able to hear and see them," Dade verified. "They can hear and see us, as well." He grabbed a cup of black coffee from the counter and headed to the sofa.

Kayla poured herself some coffee, but when she joined him, she immediately saw the dilemma. The sofa wasn't that large, and with his computer perched on the coffee table, the only way she would see the screen was to sit right next to Dade. So, that's what she did, and Kayla tried not to react when her arm brushed his.

He reacted, though.

Dade winced. And that's when her attention shot down to the bandage. "I should check that."

She didn't wait for him to agree because he wouldn't have. Kayla eased back the bandage, afraid of what she might see. The gash was an angry red color and the area around it was swollen.

"I'm taking antibiotics," Dade reminded her.

He tipped his head to the prescription bottle on the end of the coffee table. It was sitting on top of a first-aid kit. Kayla dug through the kit and came up with a tube of antibiotic cream.

"This isn't necessary," he complained.

"It is," she complained right back. "You wouldn't have been shot if you hadn't been protecting me."

That was true, and Kayla didn't regret her decision to tend his wound. But what she hadn't considered was that touching Dade posed some problems of its own.

His arm was rock-hard, and even though he wasn't heavily muscled, he was still lean and solid. A cowboy. And for some strange reason that made her smile.

"What?" Dade questioned. He dipped his head so his eyes could meet hers.

Not a good idea, either.

Because it put them breath to breath and nearly mouth to mouth.

Everything seemed to freeze. Except her heartbeat. It jolted like crazy, a reaction she quickly tried to get under control.

Dade didn't tear his attention from her. Kayla didn't move either. She just sat there, her fingers smeared with cream and poised over his arm. And in that moment, she had a terrible thought.

What would it feel like to kiss Dade?

A glimmer went through his cool gray eyes that let her know he was thinking the same thing.

"Is there a problem?" someone asked.

Kayla jerked back so fast that her neck popped.

There, on the screen, was Lieutenant Nate Ryland. She recognized him from the investigation and from his picture in the newspaper. This was Dade's fraternal twin brother. A brother who no doubt hated her to the core. And God knows what he must have seen in Dade's and her eyes.

"Kayla was checking my arm," Dade volunteered. "How much longer until the interview?"

Nate didn't answer right away. He kept his attention on Kayla. Was it disgust she saw? Or worse, was it that painful for him to look at her?

"A few more minutes," Nate finally said. "I was just checking to make sure we'd be able to see and hear you. We can," he mumbled. "By the way, Grayson had to give your location to the D.A."

"Why?" Kayla and Dade asked together.

"Winston said he had to talk to her about the trial."

Dade didn't like the idea of anyone knowing their location. Judging from Kayla's expression, neither did she. "Can't it wait?"

"Not according to Winston," Nate answered. "He has to file some papers in court today or it could jeopardize the case."

Well, Dade didn't want that, but he also didn't want to put Kayla at further risk. "Warn Winston to be careful," Dade insisted.

"I will," Nate assured him. "For now, though, I'll get Ms. Wallace in here."

"Wait," Kayla blurted out. But then she fumbled with what to say. "I'm sorry about your wife," she finally got out.

Nate stood there, his jaw muscles working against each other. It felt like an eternity. Finally, he nodded. "Thank you." And he walked out of camera range.

Kayla held her breath, wondering if Dade was going to blast her for daring to bring up the topic of Nate's dead wife. But he merely pressed the bandage back in place, reached over and muted the sound on his computer. He also handed her a tissue so she could wipe the ointment from her fingers.

"I'm very protective of my brother," Dade threw out like a warning.

"I understand." And she did. Kayla often

felt that way about Misty. "But Nate doesn't appear to be a man who needs protecting."

"Not now."

She shook her head, wondering if they were still talking about Ellie's murder.

"Things were different when we were kids," he mumbled. Dade huffed, paused, huffed again. "Something happened when Mom was pregnant with us, and Nate was born with a lot of medical problems."

Ah. She understood that, too. "So you fought his battles for him?"

"Yeah. Sometimes literally." He stared down at his hands and scraped his thumbnail over one of his knuckles. "The kids used to rag on him at school. But Nate, he was smart. A lot smarter than the kids who tried to bully him, so he could usually talk his way out of a butt whipping. Still can." Now, Dade looked at her. "He's the youngest cop in SAPD ever promoted to lieutenant. He's a big gun there."

"He's a survivor," Kayla mumbled.

Dade shrugged. "Losing Ellie nearly killed him."

And therefore it had nearly killed Dade. Kayla could see how much Dade loved his twin brother, and whether he realized it or not, he was still fighting Nate's battles. Still making sure that she wasn't a threat.

Kayla was about to assure him that she was no threat, but Dade spoke first. "Last night I did some digging into your sister's recent—"

He stopped when there was movement on the laptop screen, and Dade turned up the volume. Kayla wanted to know what Dade had been about to tell her, but she knew it would have to wait when she saw Grayson lead Misty into his office. Her sister dropped down into the chair directly in front of the webcam.

Misty did not look like a happy camper.

That was reasonable, because she was essentially in police custody and had been the entire night. Her short blond hair looked as if it hadn't been combed, and her sister wore no makeup. A rarity. It made her look much younger than twenty-seven. She looked more like a schoolgirl waiting out detention.

Misty's eyes zoomed right in on Kayla. "I can't believe you let them bring me in like this."

Kayla felt as if Misty had slapped her. All that anger in her voice, and she was glaring not at Dade or Grayson but at Kayla.

"Kayla was nearly killed," Dade responded before she could find her breath.

"Well, I didn't have anything to do with that," Misty fired back. But when she looked at Kayla again, her glare softened a little. "I'm sorry if you were almost hurt, but I'm not responsible for it."

"Not almost hurt," Dade again. "She was almost *killed* by a man named Raymond Salvetti who phoned you just a half hour before the attack."

Misty gasped. Hopefully because she was surprised by that revelation. It had to be that. Because Kayla couldn't believe that her sister would betray her. Their relationship wasn't perfect, but her sister loved her.

Kayla hoped.

Frantically shaking her head, Misty looked up at Grayson. "Someone did call me last night, and I didn't recognize the number so I let it go to voice mail. I swear, I don't know any gunmen."

"Maybe you do," Dade countered. "Think hard. Did you know Raymond Salvetti?"

Misty didn't hesitate even a second. "I don't have to think hard. I don't know anyone like that. Charles set this up. He would do anything to get to Kayla, and he probably hired this Salvetti guy."

"Yes," Kayla agreed. "But for him to do that, he had to know where I was staying. Salvetti came to the estate, Misty. He knew I was there."

Misty did more of that frantic head shaking. Kayla wanted to hold on to each one of them as the truth. "I didn't tell anyone where you were staying. You told me to keep it a secret, and I did. I swear, I did."

"How did you let Misty know that you'd be at the estate?" Grayson interrupted. He looked at Kayla. "In person? Phone? Email?"

"Phone," Kayla and Misty answered in unison. It was Kayla who continued. "Where were you when we had that conversation?" she asked Misty.

"At a bar on St. Mary's. But no one heard our conversation."

"You're sure?" Grayson pressed.

"Positive." Misty shoved her hands through her hair and groaned in frustration. "If you want to point the finger at someone other than Charles, you need to look in your own backyard. That Silver Creek D.A., Winston Calhoun, and his assistant, Alan Bowers, have been bugging me for months. Both have been trying to find Kayla. Well, I'm betting both of them knew she'd be at the estate."

It was true. Both men did know. And Kayla hadn't ruled either or both out as the leak that had led the gunman to her. Like Dade had apparently done last night, she needed to do some digging because the Rylands might not think of friends and neighbors as potential felons. But Kayla knew for a fact that Charles could be very persuasive. He had a knack for finding people's weak spots.

"Why would you think for one minute I would put Kayla in danger?" Misty demanded. She volleyed a glare between Dade and Grayson.

"Money," Dade volunteered, and he gave Kayla an *I'm-sorry* glance. "I dug into your financials last night, and I found you've recently come into some money. Ten thousand dollars to be exact."

Kayla heard the sound of shock escape from her throat. So that was what Dade had been about to tell her. Oh, God. Misty and she hadn't come from money, and even though Kayla gave her sister a monthly allowance to cover living expenses, Misty went through it as quickly as she got it. And Misty hadn't always spent the money wisely. Sometimes, she'd even used it to buy drugs. That's why Kayla hadn't just doled out more.

Ten grand was a huge sum for her sister, and Misty had to have an explanation. She just had to, and Kayla waited with her breath held.

Misty huffed. "I'm an artist," she snarled at Dade. "And I sold some paintings. That's all there is to it."

"You've got receipts for the sales, of course?" Dade remarked.

Her sister's eyes widened, and she lowered her head until she was staring down at her lap. "No, not exactly. It was a private sale. A cash deal."

Kayla's heart dropped, as well. Her sister had never made that much money from her paintings, and a sale like that should have caused Misty to call her immediately.

"I need the name and contact info for the buyer," Grayson insisted. He grabbed a notepad and pen and slid them Misty's way.

Misty's attention stayed fixed to her lap. "I don't have it, but I can get it, I suppose."

"You suppose?" Kayla questioned. She tried very hard not to get angry about such a casual comment. "Misty, someone tried to kill me and maybe Robbie, too. You have to cooperate with the police. I need answers so I can keep Robbie safe."

That got Misty's attention aimed back at the webcam. "I don't have answers!" she shouted. "The person who bought the art didn't contact me directly. He went through a friend of a friend and said he wanted the deal to be secret, that he didn't want his soon-to-be ex-wife to know he was draining their accounts." She moved closer to the screen. "Can't you see, Kayla? Someone's trying to set me up."

"Then, prove it," Dade fired back before Kayla could say anything. "Get the name of the art buyer from your friend of a friend."

Misty's forehead bunched up and she mumbled something Kayla didn't catch. "Give me twenty-four hours," she bargained. She began to chew on her thumbnail. "And I think it's time I called a lawyer."

Dade and his brother exchanged a glance. "Twenty-four hours," Grayson confirmed. "If I don't hear from you, I'm hauling you right back here, and it won't be just for questioning. I'll arrest you for obstruction of justice and any other charge I can tack on."

"Thanks a lot, Kayla," Misty snarled, and

she jumped to her feet. She practically ran out of the office.

Grayson leaned closer to the screen. "I'll call you if I find out anything."

A few seconds later, the screen went blank. Kayla's mind, however, didn't. It started to spin with plausible explanations, none of which she hoped would point to her sister's guilt.

"Charles could have set up that art deal to incriminate Misty," Kayla tossed out there. "He knows she's the only person I trust, and he might want to take that from me."

She expected Dade to counter her theory with a reminder that Misty had looked guilty of something. Or that her sister hadn't mentioned this art deal before now.

But he didn't say any of that.

Dade simply slipped his arm around her shoulder and eased her closer to him. Kayla thought about his shoulder. That this might be painful for him, but she couldn't refuse the comfort he was offering her. She'd had to stay strong for so long. All on her own. And it felt good to have a semi-ally.

"Grayson is a good cop," Dade reminded her. "He'll get to the bottom of this."

Yes. Dade was a good cop, too, and she was

afraid that *bottom* would incriminate her sister. "I feel the same way about Misty as you do about Nate. I've always protected her."

Dade stayed quiet a moment and gently rubbed his fingertips on her arm. "You're positive she didn't sell you out to Brennan?"

Kayla wanted to be angry that he would even ask. After all, she'd had no trouble feeling that anger during Misty's interview. But it wasn't anger she felt this time.

It was fear for what Misty could have done.

"Charles could have manipulated her," Kayla suggested. "He could have made her believe that telling him my whereabouts would be the only way to keep me alive."

"But wouldn't she have admitted that to you, especially after I told her that you'd nearly been killed?"

Kayla hoped that would be true, but she had to shake her head. "She might be too afraid to tell me."

She braced herself for Dade to huff or roll his eyes, but he didn't. Maybe because he had five siblings, he understood the sometimes-delicate dynamics of family.

"Misty doesn't know how bad things were with Preston and Charles," Kayla continued. "She knows I witnessed some illegal activity.

That I overheard conversations about money laundering and such. But Misty believes those were rare occurrences. They weren't."

Dade stayed quiet a moment. "Exactly how much did you witness?"

"Too much," she mumbled. "I overheard and saw enough to convict Charles of dozens of felonies."

"Good thing, too, because I doubt there's any physical evidence to nail him."

"There used to be," Kayla admitted. "He had files at his office and heaven knows what stashed in safe-deposit boxes under fake names." She had to take a deep breath because that was a reminder of just how dangerous her former father-in-law was and continued to be.

Dade turned slightly so they were directly facing each other. "Protecting Robbie and you comes first. I can't put Misty or anyone else ahead of that, understand?"

"Yes." It's exactly what she wanted Dade to do—to protect her son at all cost.

And Dade would. She didn't have to second-guess that.

Mercy.

How much her life had changed in these short hours. Just yesterday, she thought of

Dade and all the Rylands as the enemy, but she no longer felt that way about Dade.

That could be a major mistake.

"Yeah," she heard him say and realized he was studying her eyes as if he knew exactly what she was thinking. Maybe he did because he looked away, cursed and mumbled something.

"What?" she asked.

He cursed again. "This," he answered.

This was bad. Because Dade turned back to her, leaned in and touched his mouth to hers. It was quick. And dirty. It packed a punch of a full-fledged French kiss.

"Hell," he mumbled. "If I'm breaking the rules, I might as well break 'em hard."

And he did.

His hand went around the back of her neck and he dragged her to him. Not just the lip contact but some body-to-body contact as well. Her breasts landed against his toned chest muscles.

Oh, he was good. Too good. His mouth blazed against her and sent a jolt of fire through all the wrong parts of her body.

She'd been right about Dade. He could melt chrome with that mouth and seduce her straight to his bed. Something that couldn't happen.

Kayla repeated that to herself. Several times.

Finally, she managed to pull back. Or maybe she was successful only because Dade pulled back as well.

"There are about a hundred reasons why that can't happen again," he insisted. And he inched away from her so they were no longer touching.

Kayla couldn't argue with that, and she could even add some reasons of her own. "I can't get involved because my last relationship nearly destroyed me. Besides, when you look at me, you'll always think of Nate's dead wife."

He made a sound of agreement.

And then Kayla heard another sound.

One that she hadn't expected to hear. Apparently, neither had Dade because he sprang from the sofa, and in the same motion, he drew his gun from his shoulder holster. He hurried to the window, and Kayla followed, but Dade only pushed her behind him.

"Hell," Dade mumbled. "We have a visitor."

Chapter 7

Dade drew his gun and pushed Kayla behind him. No one should be here, but there was a black four-door sedan barreling up the dirt road toward the ranch house.

"Who is it?" Kayla asked. Her voice wasn't just trembling, it was downright shaking.

Dade kept his gun and his attention nailed to the car, and it didn't take him long to figure out who their *visitor* was. Or rather *visitors*. Because he instantly recognized the two men who exited the car when it came to a stop in front of the house.

"It's the D.A., Winston Calhoun, and the assistant D.A., Alan Bowers," he said.

She drew in a hard breath. "They're here already?"

"Is everything okay?" Connie called out to them.

"Yeah," Dade answered, but he had no idea if that was the truth. "Just stay put with Robbie."

When he started across the yard, Winston ducked his head down, probably because of the icy wind. He carried a leather briefcase and was dressed for work in an iron-gray business suit that matched the color of his hair and the winter sky. He was a good twenty years older than Dade, and Dade had known the man his entire life.

He couldn't say the same for Alan.

The thirty-something-year-old had moved to Silver Creek about a year and a half ago when he'd gotten the job at the D.A.'s office. He was lanky to the point of being wiry, with hair so blond that he looked more at home on the beach than he did in cowboy country. Like his boss, Alan wore a suit, so this obviously wasn't a social call.

When the men made it to the porch, Dade reholstered his gun, disengaged the security system and opened the door. "This had better be important," he snarled.

Winston spared him a glance, but his dark eyes went to Kayla. Yeah. Something was definitely wrong, but Winston didn't say a word until both Alan and he had stepped inside.

"Charles Brennan's lawyers just requested a trial delay," Winston announced.

Kayla didn't make a sound, but Dade could feel her reaction. Every muscle in her body tensed.

"Please tell me he won't get it," Dade insisted.

Alan lifted his bony shoulder, and Winston shook his head. Dade just cursed. Kayla and Robbie sure as hell didn't need this.

"You could have told us this over the phone," Dade pointed out. "Rather than risk someone following you."

Alan's mouth tightened. Probably because he was insulted that Dade had just slammed him for what Dade considered to be an unnecessary visit that could turn out to be a big-time security risk.

Winston, however, had no visible reaction. "This visit is important," he declared. "And for the record, no one followed us. We were careful."

Winston set his briefcase on the table near

the door and extracted a manila file. "I need to get Kayla's signature on the statement she gave me over the phone two days ago." He handed her both the file and pen.

"Of course." Kayla's voice was still shaky and so was her hand. And Dade knew why. The statement and her signature would be needed if for some reason Kayla couldn't testify.

In other words, if Dade failed to do his job and Brennan killed her.

"I'd like to read through this first," Kayla said, her attention already on the first page. She sank onto the sofa.

"It's all there," Alan informed her. He made a nervous gesture toward the papers. "We just need your signature so we can leave."

Kayla lifted her eyes. Met his. "I'd still prefer to read it."

Dade was about to second that and even insist on it. Not because he didn't trust Winston but because this entire visit was well beyond making him feel uncomfortable. However, before Dade could say anything, Winston latched onto his arm and pulled him aside. Alan stayed near Kayla.

"We haven't been able to link the dead gunman, Salvetti, to Brennan," Winston whispered. "But we have been able to link Brennan to Danny Flynn, the guy the gunman called. Flynn did some handyman work at Brennan's estate."

None of this surprised Dade. "Any proof that Flynn orchestrated the attack last night?"

"No. But get this—Brennan says Flynn's trying to set him up because he fired him."

Of course Brennan would say that. He would say and do anything to cover his butt.

Dade heard Robbie make a sound. A squeal, followed by a fussy protest. And Kayla nearly jumped off the sofa.

"I'll check on him," Dade told her. Best for her to finish reading the statement so he could get Winston and Alan out of there.

Dade headed down the hall, and it didn't take him long to spot the baby. Connie had him in a snug protective grip, but Robbie clearly wanted to get down. Dade went closer, and when the baby reached out for him, Dade pulled him into his arms.

Without thinking, he brushed a kiss on Robbie's forehead.

That was something he often did to his niece, Kimmie, but he regretted it now. That kiss earned him a raised eyebrow from the nanny who clearly didn't trust him. Robbie, on the other hand, was loaded with trust. He babbled something to Dade and dropped his head on Dade's shoulder.

Heck.

Dade didn't want to feel the warmth of holding this child in his arms. Because Kayla was still his family's enemy. There couldn't be anything between them.

Well, except for his feelings for her son.

And that kiss, of course.

But Dade was reasonably sure he'd be disgusted with himself about that later. Too bad the attraction he felt for her kept putting off that *later*.

Dade tried to hand Robbie back to the nanny, but when the baby fussed again, Dade kept hold of him and returned to the living room to check on Kayla. When she spotted them, Dade got another raised eyebrow. Dade looked at Robbie to see his reaction, and the little boy gave him a big toothy grin. Dade couldn't help but grin back.

"I'm finished." Kayla scrawled her signature on the last page of the statement and handed both the pages and the pen back to Winston. She didn't waste even a second taking Robbie from him.

Dade had expected those raised eyebrows

from their guests, but he was a little miffed that Kayla would have that reaction, especially because they'd set fire to each other's lips just minutes earlier.

"I'll let you know if Brennan gets the trial delay," Winston assured them. He tipped his head in a farewell gesture, and the two attorneys headed to the door.

Dade followed them, closing the door behind them and resetting the security alarm. He turned to ask Kayla about that raised eyebrow reaction, but she spoke before he could.

"You trust both of those men?" she asked. It didn't seem like an accusation exactly, but there was concern dripping from her voice.

"I trust Winston." But then he had to shrug. "I don't really know Alan. Why, did you get bad vibes from him?"

"From both of them," she corrected. "But then I'm getting bad vibes from almost everyone."

He stared at her. "Even from me? I noticed you didn't care for my holding your son."

She opened her mouth as if she might leap to dispute it, but then Kayla shook her head. "It's not that." And she repeated it. "Your brothers hate me, and I don't want to do anything that would hurt your relationship with them. I figured the D.A. would report back anything and everything he saw here."

Oh, he would. Maybe Alan, too. But Grayson had already seen the close contact between Kayla and him at the start of the interview with Misty. Grayson wasn't stupid, and he no doubt had already noticed what was simmering between Kayla and him.

"It might be too late to do that kind of damage control." Dade went closer, caught onto Robbie's foot and gave it a jiggle. He was rewarded with a grin.

"Is everything okay?" Connie asked from the hall.

"Yes," Kayla quickly answered. "I'll keep Robbie with me for a while and give you some time for reading."

The nanny made a sound of approval, but Dade doubted she'd get much quality reading time. The attack from the night before was too fresh on all their minds.

Kayla grabbed the diaper bag from the coffee table, took out several small stuffed animals and sank down onto the floor with Robbie so he could play. Dade checked out the window.

Nothing, thank God. Maybe it would stay that way.

He maneuvered himself so he could keep watch but sat on the floor along with them. Robbie seemed to approve because he handed Dade a blue horse and then laughed when Dade made a neighing sound.

"You're good with kids," Kayla said sounding more than a little surprised.

Dade shrugged and took out his wallet. He opened it to show her a picture of his thirteen-month-old niece, Kimmie. The picture was there all right, front and center, but something fell out.

A tarnished silver concho.

Kayla grabbed it before it could hit the floor and stared at it. The concho was a blast from the past that he didn't need, and Dade had forgotten it was even there.

"It's the symbol for the Ryland ranch." The double back-to-back Rs were prominently displayed. "My father gave me and each of my brothers one before…well, before he left."

One look in Kayla's suddenly sympathetic eyes, and he knew she'd already heard at least bits and pieces of this tragic story. Boone Ryland had run off and abandoned his six sons twenty years ago, and that had been just the beginning of things gone wrong for what was left of the Rylands.

"Twenty years," Dade mumbled, "and the gossip hasn't died down."

Kayla didn't deny she'd heard gossip. She reached out, touched his arm and rubbed gently. Her touch was warm and curled through him, but it was also a reminder that the events twenty years ago would always be a stab to his heart.

He took the concho from her, shoved it back into his wallet and put it away. Out of sight but never out of mind.

Kayla cleared her throat and eased Robbie back into her lap when he tried to crawl away. "Nate's child is your only niece or nephew?" she asked.

Dade was a hundred-percent thankful for the change in subject. "Yeah, but Grayson and his wife have one on the way." He kept his attention fastened to the window.

"Grayson looks as if he'd be a good father," she remarked. Her forehead bunched up. "Not your other brother, though."

He knew exactly which brother she meant. "Mason." And he couldn't disagree with her. "Mason is a hard man to figure out. Hard on himself. And others. After our dad left, Mason took his concho, shot it with a .38 and then nailed what was left of it to his bedroom wall. Said it was the first thing he wanted to see when he got up in the morning so he'd remember how much he hated the old man."

When Kayla didn't say anything, he glanced at her. Her mouth had dropped open a little. "That doesn't sound...healthy."

"Not much about our past was," he admitted. He sure hadn't planned on spilling his guts this way, but he didn't stop, either. "Plain and simple, my father gave us those conchos to relieve his guilt, and then he destroyed us, especially our mom. She committed suicide on Grayson's eighteenth birthday and left a note begging him to keep the family together."

Kayla touched his arm again. Probably to give him another of those soothing rubs, but Dade moved away. "Grayson succeeded."

"Yeah, I guess. He's happy now anyway." One of six wasn't exactly a good track record, but before Grayson's wife, Eve, had come back into his life a few months earlier, the Rylands had been batting a thousand in the bad-relationship department.

Kayla stayed quiet a moment. "So what about you—have you always kept your concho in your wallet?"

This wasn't a story he was used to tell-

ing, not out loud anyway, although he remembered it like it was yesterday. "When we
were fourteen, Nate and I threw ours in Silver Creek. But like a bad penny, mine turned
up. Grayson's wife found it about a week ago
when she was out taking some pictures for a
newspaper article she's working on."

Kayla's mouth dropped open again. "She
found it after all these years?"

He shook his head and waved her off.
"Don't go there. This isn't some kind of cosmic sign for me to forgive my father." Dade
bit back the profanity of what he really wanted
to call Boone Ryland because Robbie was in
the room. "It was just blind luck she found
it, that's all. And first chance I get, I'll toss it
right back in the creek. Heck, maybe the Gulf
of Mexico. Doubt anyone would find it then."

The silence came. Of course it did. He'd
just saddled a mountain of old baggage on
Kayla. Right about now she was probably
thinking he needed some big-time therapy,
and she was no doubt regretting that kiss, too.

"Don't throw the concho away." Her voice
was a whisper now. "Give it to me."

Dade was sure he looked at her as if she'd
sprouted horns. "Why?"

She flashed him one of those half smiles,

the ones that weren't of the happy variety. "So I have something to remember the man who saved my and my son's lives."

Good grief. That wasn't a good reason because it seemed intimate. Or something. It definitely didn't seem *right*.

"Plus," she continued. The smile was gone now, and her chin came up. Second-guessing her request, he figured. "If you want cosmic justice, what better way to get it than to give your enemy the guilt gift from a father you despise?"

Dade just stared at her, and she stared back. Robbie did, too, as if he was trying to figure out what was going on.

"Forget I said that," Kayla added. She tried to chuckle. Failed. "I won't need anything to remember you."

Yeah. Dade felt the same about her. Kayla would be in his dreams—hot, uncomfortable dreams—long after this assignment ended. It'd been a while since he'd wanted a woman as much as he wanted Kayla.

Dade could already feel his hands on her. Could taste her. Could hear the sounds she'd make when he was deep inside her. And that hard ache went through his body and begged him to kick this attraction up a notch.

But he couldn't. Because of her safety. And because of that cute little kid staring up at him.

Dade stood and took out his wallet. Then, the concho. He tossed it into Kayla's lap. Quick, like stripping off a bandage that had been in place way too long.

She picked up the silver-dollar-sized concho the way a person would handle fine crystal and closed her fingers around it when Robbie reached for it, as well. She gave her baby a kiss instead.

Yet another too-intimate moment that he shouldn't be experiencing with Kayla. He'd be thankful when this trial was over so he could put some distance between them.

And Dade was almost sure he believed that.

"A car," Kayla said at the same moment Dade heard the sound of the engine.

Hell. What now? Maybe Winston had driven back to tell them that Brennan had gotten the delay he'd requested. If so, Dade was going to give them instructions on how to use a phone to relay information.

Dade hurried to the window next to the door and looked out. He groaned, but inside his reaction was much worse.

Kayla latched onto Robbie and hugged him close to her body. "Who is it?"

"It's trouble," Dade let her know, and when he drew his gun he was afraid this time he might have to use it.

Chapter 8

Kayla tried to brace herself for the worst, and the worst would be Charles. However, he wasn't the person who stepped from the car.

It was her sister, Misty.

Dade glanced back at her as if expecting an explanation, but Kayla didn't have one. "I didn't tell anyone including Misty, where we were staying."

"Well, someone did, unless it's blind luck she found her way out here," he snarled. "Go to the bedroom and wait. Keep Robbie quiet if you can. Maybe she's just on a fishing expedition and doesn't actually know you're here."

Kayla was about to insist that Misty was

no threat. Old habits died hard, and she had a lifetime habit of defending Misty. But the truth was their location had likely been compromised. Now the question was how?

"Carrie Collins," Dade spat out like profanity.

It took Kayla a moment to realize why Dade had said the woman's name, but then she spotted the tall brunette who got out of the driver's side of the car. It was the paramedic who'd come to her estate right after the shooting.

"Your sister knows Carrie?" Dade asked, his attention fastened to the two women making their way to the porch.

"I don't think so." Yet, here they were together.

What was going on?

Kayla shoved the concho into her pocket and hurried to the hall where Connie was waiting. The nanny had no doubt heard the car engine and was wondering if they were about to be attacked again.

She handed Robbie to Connie. "I'll be back after I talk to my sister."

And by God, Misty better have some answers.

By the time Kayla returned to the living

room, Dade was talking on his cell. She didn't know who he had called, but he clearly wasn't happy. He had such a grip on the phone that she was surprised it didn't crush to powder, and his eyes were narrowed to slits.

"Who says I'm at the Wellman ranch?" Dade barked. He paused, then cursed. "How the hell did you manage to follow Winston?"

Kayla's stomach dropped. If her sister and this medic had followed the D.A., then Charles's hired guns could have done the same. Oh, mercy. This had just gone from bad to worse.

As if he'd declared war on it, Dade paused the security system and threw open the door. Carrie tried to push her way in, but Dade blocked her.

"I need to check your arm," Carrie insisted. "You could get an infection. Or worse."

"My arm is fine," Dade insisted right back, and he jerked away from Carrie when she tried to check the bandage that was visible just beneath the sleeve of his black T-shirt.

Carrie's eyes narrowed as well, and she shot Kayla a glare. Kayla ignored it and saved her glare for Misty, who was practically standing behind the much taller Carrie.

"Why did you come?" Kayla asked her sister.

"Why?" Misty stepped to Carrie's side. "Because you believe I tried to kill you. I had to see you, to convince you of the obvious. I would never take money from someone who wants to hurt you."

It certainly sounded convincing, and Kayla wanted to believe her, but there was the issue of the money that Misty had recently acquired. There was also her sister's mere presence.

"Why did you come here?" Kayla asked. Again, she had to dodge a glare from Carrie. "You must have realized that someone could have followed you."

"No one did," Carrie snapped, and she repeated it to Dade. "I'm not stupid, Dade. I know how to watch my back—and yours."

"Winston was certain no one had followed him, either," Dade informed them. "But you somehow managed it. How?"

Carrie huffed, and her glare softened. "I figured Winston or Alan would be out to see you sooner or later, so I kept an eye on the parking lot at the D.A.'s office. I got lucky and saw them leave."

"You did all that so you could check on my

arm?" Dade didn't sound happy about that. Or convinced that Carrie was telling the truth.

That put some fire back in her eyes. "I care about you," Carrie snarled under her breath. And then she put that snarl into the look she gave Kayla.

Oh, so that's what was going on. Carrie had a thing for Dade. That was, well, reasonable. After all, Dade was a hot guy and no doubt a prime catch. Still, it made Kayla uncomfortable, and she didn't want to explore why she didn't like Carrie going to extremes to check on Dade.

Kayla walked closer until she was side-by-side with Dade and snared her sister's attention. "Were you watching the D.A.'s parking lot, too?"

The seconds crawled by before Misty answered. "Yes, and when Carrie spotted me, we got to talking. I asked her to bring me out here with her."

"She demanded I bring her," Carrie clarified to Dade. "I agreed finally because I didn't want her to do something stupid by trying to follow me."

Kayla figured the *something stupid* had already happened.

"You put Robbie in danger by coming

here," Kayla told Misty. Her sister opened her mouth, but Kayla spoke right over her. "We can talk about your innocence after the trial. After Robbie is safe. But for now, I need you just to back off and stay away from us."

Misty flinched, and her eyes actually watered. Because Kayla had never seen Misty cry anything but crocodile tears, she had to wonder if these were genuine. If so, Kayla would owe her a huge apology. Later. After the trial.

"You both need to leave," Dade said. And it wasn't a suggestion. It was an order. He started to close the door, but Carrie caught onto it.

However, the woman didn't look at Dade. She looked at Kayla. "You don't even remember me, do you?"

Kayla lifted her shoulder. "You were at the estate last night."

"Before that. I was with Preston the night you two met."

Kayla hadn't expected the woman to say that, and with so much already on her mind, it took her a few moments to remember that night.

"A charity fundraiser in San Antonio,"

Carrie added. "I was talking to Preston, and you interrupted us."

Yes, she remembered meeting them, and she vaguely recalled a woman next to Preston. Until now she'd had no idea it was Carrie. "A friend interrupted you," Kayla corrected, "so she could introduce me to Preston."

At the time, Kayla had thought it was one of the best moments of her life. And she continued to think that until she got to know the abusive man behind that million-dollar smile.

"Does this have anything to do with the trial or Kayla's safety?" Dade demanded. He clicked on his phone. "Because I have security arrangements to make."

"Yes, it does have something to do with the trial." Carrie had a death grip on the door to keep Dade from closing it. "Kayla was bad news then, and she's bad news now. She went to that fundraiser to meet a rich guy, and she succeeded. She didn't care that Preston and I were dating. She just moved right in on him."

Stunned by Carrie's accusation, Kayla pulled back her shoulders. "I wasn't aware you were seeing Preston. He didn't mention it."

"And I'm sure you didn't ask." Carrie paused and glanced away. "Preston ended things with me that night, and I figure you had plenty to do with that. I know your type, and I know you would have said and done anything to snag a man like him. All that money, all that power. You wanted it, and you didn't care who you pushed aside to get it."

Kayla could only shake her head. "You know nothing about me," she insisted.

"Kayla's right—you don't," Misty agreed. "And I didn't come out here so you could attack my sister."

Carrie ignored them and switched her attention to Dade. "Kayla could get you killed. You must know she had something to do with that attack last night. Why else would the gunman have called her?"

Because Kayla was right against Dade's back, she felt his muscles go stiff. "How did you know about that call?"

Carrie's eyes widened. For just a second. And then she shrugged. "I heard someone talking about it. Don't remember who." Her stare drilled into Dade. "How else would I have known? You're not accusing me of anything, are you?"

Dade cursed. "No, but I am telling you for the last time to leave." And to make sure that happened, he slammed the door in their faces.

"I'm sorry," Kayla said at the exact moment Dade said it, too.

Kayla managed a frustrated groan. Dade skipped the groan and made a call. To his brother, no doubt. They had to get out of there fast, now that seemingly everyone in Silver Creek knew their location.

While Dade was on the phone, Kayla looked out the window to make sure their guests did indeed drive away. Her sister gave her one last glance before she got in the car. The glance was definitely one of disapproval. Maybe because Kayla hadn't welcomed her with open arms. Maybe because Misty thought Kayla should have defended her more.

It didn't matter which.

The bottom line was that she couldn't trust her sister. Coming here had been irresponsible at best and at worst, it had endangered Robbie.

Dade ended his call and looked out the window just as Carrie and Misty were driving away. "Get your things ready. Grayson will be out in a half hour to escort us to our ranch."

"Your ranch?" she questioned. "Your brothers aren't going to like that."

"My brothers are all lawmen, and they'd never put their personal feelings above the badge." But that troubled expression let her know that this would not be a laid-back visit. "It's only temporary, until we can make arrangements for another safe house."

Kayla turned to tell Connie the news, but she stopped. So did Dade, and he shook his head. "Think back to last night," he told her. "Was the gunman's phone call mentioned while Carrie was still there?"

Kayla tried to pick through the details of that nightmare. "I don't think so." And that led her to her next question. "You suspect her of something?"

He shook his head. "Don't know yet. I don't like that she brought up her connection to your late-husband."

Neither did Kayla. "She seemed to think I was horning in on her possible relationship with Preston. And with you."

Dade didn't deny it, and the suddenly tight jaw muscles confirmed it. "Carrie and I were together, but things ended between us months ago."

Kayla didn't doubt that Dade had ended the relationship. Nor did she doubt Carrie still had feelings for Dade. She only hoped that

Carrie wouldn't risk their safety all for the sake of getting Dade back into her life.

"I'll tell Connie we're leaving soon," Kayla let him know. But the nanny had obviously overheard the news because she was already packing their things.

Kayla started to help, but then she heard Dade's phone ring again. She hurried back to the living room to make sure nothing else had gone wrong.

"Kayla's not available," Dade said. His voice and his face were tense, and she walked closer, wondering who had caused this reaction.

"Do your slimy lawyers know you called me?" Dade asked whoever was on the other end of the line. "Brennan," he mouthed to her.

Oh, God. She'd already had enough for one day without adding him to the mix. Why was the devil himself calling Dade?

Dade's mouth tightened even more. So did the grip he had on the tiny cell phone. "That sounds like a threat."

Threat. That word slammed through her like a heavyweight's fist. Charles was liberal with his threats, she had grown accustomed to them, but how dare he call now after nearly succeeding in killing her?

She marched across the room and held out her hand. "I need to talk to him."

Dade was shaking his head when she ripped the phone from his hand. "What do you want?" Kayla demanded from Charles.

"Kayla." Charles said her name in that sappy sweet way that only he could manage. "You're a hard woman to reach. I've been calling all around, trying to find you. Imagine my surprise to learn you're with one of the Ryland boys. My advice? Sleep with one eye open because the Rylands would love to slit your pretty little throat."

"What…do…you…want?" Kayla paused between each word because she was fighting to hold on to her composure. She wanted to scream. She wanted to reach through the phone and slap this vile man.

"I called to make sure Robbie was okay." The sappiness went down a notch.

"Well, he's not." She turned away from Dade when he tried to take the phone, but she did hold it so he could hear. "He's in danger because of you. Because of the assassins you hired to kill me."

"Kayla…" Silence, for a few seconds. "My differences with you would never extend to my grandson. Besides, I didn't hire any assassins."

She didn't believe him for a minute and judging from Dade's snarl, neither did he. "What kind of sick man endangers a baby just so he won't have to go to jail?"

Charles cursed. "I didn't endanger him, but I intend to find out who did." And with that, he ended the call, leaving Kayla to wonder what the heck had just happened.

"He's trying to trick me into believing he wasn't behind that attack last night," she mumbled.

Dade eased the phone from her hand and hit the end call button. He also turned so he could keep watch out the window. "Before that attack, had Brennan done anything to put Robbie at risk?"

Kayla didn't want to think of the past year or the months before that when she was pregnant, but she forced herself to go back. To the bad memories. To the beatings that Preston had delivered. To the verbal abuse from Charles.

"No," Kayla answered. "When Charles learned I was pregnant, he seemed happy. And he was even happier when he learned I was carrying a boy. He warned Preston not to hit me when I was pregnant because he didn't want to risk a miscarriage."

That confession cut through her because it was a reminder of the life she'd led. Trapped in hell. She was so ashamed of what she'd allowed to happen.

"Don't cry," she heard Dade say, and that's when she realized there were tears in her eyes.

Kayla cursed the tears. She was tired of crying and just as tired of breaking down in front of Dade.

"I'm not a wuss," she mumbled.

"Never thought you were." He huffed and pulled her into his arms. "Shh," he whispered, his breath brushing against her hair.

It felt so good to have him hold her like this. His arms were warm and safe, but she couldn't do this. Dade was nothing like Preston, but she had to stand on her own two feet.

And that's why Kayla stepped back.

Dade looked at her, frowned and hooked his arm around her waist. He snapped her right back to him. "I'm offering you a shoulder to cry on. That's it. No strings attached."

"Oh, there are strings." And she hadn't meant to say that aloud. Dade was looking out the window, keeping watch, but she waited until his eyes angled back to her. "This attraction has strings."

"Yeah," he admitted. He brushed his mouth over hers. "I wish I could do something about that, but I can't. I want you. You want me. You're scared of a relationship, and I don't want my brothers hating you any more than they already do."

Kayla took a deep breath. "So our decision should be easy. We keep our hands off each other."

He raised an eyebrow because his hands were already on her. And he wasn't backing away. Dade leaned down and put his mouth on hers again. It was just a touch, but it blazed right through her, leaving her breathless. Making her want more.

Kayla couldn't have more. Not now. Not ever.

She put her hands on his chest to push herself back. To put some much-needed distance between his hands and her body.

But a sound stopped her cold.

Chapter 9

The blast ripped through the house.

Dade automatically drew his gun, but this wasn't another visitor. Nor were shots being fired.

This was an explosion.

"Go to Robbie," Dade told Kayla, but she was already heading in that direction.

Dade pressed the emergency response button on his phone to alert the dispatcher of a problem, and he hurried to the side of the window and looked out, not sure of what he might see. But what he saw sent his stomach to the floor.

His SUV was a fireball.

Dade knew this wasn't some kind of freak accident. No. Someone had put an explosive device in it. But Dade couldn't see that *someone*. He checked the yard and the pasture on both sides of the SUV.

No one.

It was too much to hope that the person had set the explosive and then left. In all probability, the bomber had moved to the back or sides of the house where he'd be out of sight.

And was ready to attack.

Dade did a quick check of the security system to make sure it was armed. It was. And he hurried to the kitchen so he'd have a view of the backyard and the outbuildings.

"Take Robbie and Connie and get into the bathroom," he yelled out to Kayla.

Judging from the sound of the footsteps, Kayla was already doing that. Dade hoped it would be enough to keep them safe.

He peered around the window frame and into the backyard. He didn't spot anyone, but there were a lot of places to hide. Two barns, trees and even several old watering troughs in the corral area. Because the troughs were metal, that would make them an ideal place to hide and then launch an attack.

But what was this attack about?

Had Brennan sent someone to kill Kayla?

That didn't feel right. Because if he'd wanted her dead, he could have instructed the bomber to toss the explosive closer to the house. Of course, that would have endangered Robbie. So, maybe this was some kind of ruse to get them to run. The thought had no sooner crossed his mind when he caught the scent.

Smoke.

Dade couldn't see any flames, but he could certainly smell it, and threads of thin gray smoke started to seep through the tiny gaps around the back door.

"The house is on fire!" Kayla yelled a split-second before the smoke detectors went off.

Their situation had just gone from bad to worse, because Dade knew how this was going down. He had to get Kayla and the others out of the house. Outside. Where that bomber-arsonist was waiting for them.

Later, he would kick himself for allowing this to happen, but for now he needed to take some measures to keep them all alive.

With his gun ready, Dade hurried to the other side of the house where Kayla and Connie were waiting in the doorway of the bathroom. Kayla had Robbie in her arms, but the baby was kicking and fussing.

"The fire," Kayla said, pointing through the open doorway of the second bedroom.

Dade could see the flames now. Bright orangey red, and they were licking up the side of the house. There wasn't much time.

"We have to get out," he told them, although it was clear from their faces they already knew that. The trick was *how* to get them out.

He snatched a damp towel from a hanging bar and tossed it over Robbie. Maybe it would give him some protection. "Stay low and follow me. Hurry," Dade added.

There were two exits, front and back. Plus the windows, but he couldn't use those because it would take too long to get them all out. Speed was important now. They had to hit the ground running and get behind cover. Not easy to do with a baby in tow. Maybe they would get lucky, and Dade could hold off an assassin until backup arrived.

Thank God Grayson was already on the way.

Keeping watch, Dade led them back through the living room, but he stopped to grab a backup handgun from his overnight bag. Unfortunately, they might need it.

"I can shoot," Kayla insisted, and she

passed Robbie to the nanny so she could take the gun.

Dade wanted to say no, that he didn't want her to have to fend off an assassin, but right now he needed all the help he could get.

"We're going out front," Dade let them know.

It could be a wrong call. A gunman could be out there waiting, but his gut told him their attacker would be expecting them to leave through the back, as far away from that burning SUV as they could get.

Kayla's breath came even faster. Maybe because of the smoke that was drifting through the room. "What then?"

Another gamble. "I go first. Then Connie and the baby. We keep them between us." Protecting them from gunfire. He hoped. "Once we're off the porch, run out the gate to the right of what's left of the SUV and then drop down. There's a deep ditch out there, and we'll use it for cover."

Kayla gave a shaky nod, one that Connie repeated, but neither looked at all confident in his plan. Robbie peeked out at him, his head and body covered with the thick towel, and it nearly broke Dade's heart to think of the baby in danger. This wasn't right. No child should be in this position.

"It'll be okay, buddy," Dade whispered to the baby. He gave Kayla one last look. She was terrified, her hands shaking, but he saw the determination there, too. She was a fighter, and that was exactly what he needed right now.

Dade hurried to the door and threw it open, not bothering to disarm the security system. Hopefully, the alarm would unnerve their attacker in some small way. He looked out, didn't see anyone waiting to attack, so he motioned for them to follow.

The blast of cold air came right at them the moment they stepped onto the porch. It was mixed with the stench of the fire, and the smoke from both the flames and the SUV. The SUV was already a goner, and it wouldn't be long before the wood frame house was reduced to ashes.

Dade moved quickly, maneuvering Connie and Robbie onto the porch and then the steps. Kayla was right behind them, not as close as he wanted but that's because she was keeping watch behind them. Good move. Because their attacker could come through the back of the house and ambush them.

"Hurry," Dade instructed Connie even though he doubted she could hear him over the clanging security alarms.

With Robbie in her arms, Connie stepped down into the ditch. Dade looked back to motion to Kayla to hurry as well, but she wasn't looking at him. Her body snapped to the right side of the house. So did her aim.

And she fired.

Everything happened fast. Dade got a split-second glimpse of the person dressed head to toe in black before Kayla's bullet sent the gunman ducking for cover on the opposite side of the house where the fire was blazing.

Kayla held her position. Her weapon raised and ready.

"Get down here!" Dade shouted to her.

He had already aimed at their attacker, and it didn't take long before the guy lifted his head again. He fired right at Dade.

Kayla yelled for him to get down. Dade did the same to her again, but she didn't move until a bullet came her way.

Hell.

She was out there in the open, too easy of a target. And she seemed to be frozen. Or maybe she was trying to use herself as a diversion so the gunman wouldn't send any bullets toward Robbie and Connie.

He didn't intend to let Kayla sacrifice herself.

Dade glanced at Connie to make sure she was deep in the ditch. She was. And she was using her own body to protect Robbie. They were away from the house fire and the SUV. The baby was as safe as he could be, so Dade did something about making sure Kayla didn't get killed.

He sprinted to her and hooked his arm around her waist. But he wasn't fast enough.

The bullets came flying right at them.

Even with the deafening noise of the security alarm, Kayla had no trouble hearing the shots. Or seeing their attacker as he leaned out and fired.

She returned fire just as Dade pulled her off the porch and to the ground. He scrambled to get them to the side of the house. Opposite the gunman and so close to the fire that she could feel the heat from the flames.

But she was also yards away from her precious baby.

Kayla wanted to run to Connie and him. She needed to make sure they were all right, but if she stepped out, their attacker would kill her. She wasn't afraid for her own life, but if she got killed, she wouldn't be there to protect Robbie.

"Keep watch behind us," Dade shouted to her.

Oh, God.

She hadn't even considered that the gunman might run to the back of the house and shoot at them through the flames and smoke. If he did that, at least he wouldn't be near the ditch, but again she couldn't take the risk of Dade and her being gunned down. She turned, putting her back up against Dade's, and Kayla held her breath, waiting. And praying.

Somehow, she had to get her baby safely out of this.

She cursed herself for coming back to testify, but sooner or later it would have come down to this. A confrontation with Charles was inevitable, and she'd only delayed things when she went into hiding.

The winter wind shifted and sent the black smoke right at them, spreading it all around— not just the house but also the yard. The gunman could use it as a shield, but worse, the smoke burned her throat and lungs. Kayla started to cough. Not good. Because that would give away their position.

"We have to move," Dade insisted.

Kayla knew he was right, but there seemed no place to go. The fire was directly behind them, and if they went into the front yard, the gunman would pick them off. That left the side. No fence. No buildings they could duck behind. However, there were some pecan trees about thirty feet away. If they could get to those, they could use the trees for protection and still be able to see the ditch.

"Stay low and move fast," Dade instructed, and he tipped his head to the trees.

Kayla nodded and prayed they could make it. Dade gave her one last glance, and he seemed to be trying to apologize to her. But Kayla was the one who'd gotten them into this mess. She hoped later she would have the chance to tell Dade how sorry she was for that.

"Now," Dade ordered. He, too, was coughing now, and she hoped the move would at least put them out of the smoke's path.

Each step was a victory, and she counted them off in her head while keeping watch over her shoulder. They only made it six steps before she saw the figure emerge from the smoke. She and Dade just kept running, but Kayla kept watch behind them.

At first their attacker seemed to be part of the smoke itself, but she realized that's because he wore black clothes. Only his face was visible. Definitely a man, tall and thin, and he had the cold, hard look of a killer.

The man took aim at them and fired. Just as Dade dragged her to the ground. The dirt was like ice, and the cold and adrenaline slammed through her. Her heart rate spiked when the bullet slammed into the ground just inches from her.

Dade pivoted and fired at the shooter. He didn't waste any time. He latched onto her wrist with his left hand and yanked her hard, shoving her behind the tree. Dade followed, readjusting his aim, but he didn't fire.

Kayla peered out from the pecan tree. She could no longer see the gunman, but thankfully the smoke wasn't obliterating her view of the ditch. Or the road—where she saw the approaching vehicle.

"There's a truck," she said to Dade.

His gaze whipped in that direction, but Kayla pinned her attention to the area where she'd last seen their attacker.

Where the heck was he?

As menacing as it was to see him step out of that wall of smoke, not knowing where he was chilled her to the bone. She kept her gun ready and tried to steady both her heart and her trembling hands.

"It's Grayson's truck," she heard Dade say.

Relief flooded through her, but it was short-lived. That's because a bullet slammed into the tree just inches from her. Kayla jumped back, bashing into Dade, but both of them somehow managed to keep hold of their guns.

Volleying glances between the direction of that last shot and the road, Kayla spotted the Silver Creek patrol truck that had come to a stop just twenty yards or so from the house. Grayson was behind the wheel and he was alone. She wished he'd brought the entire deputy force, but at the moment she would take whatever she could get.

"Keep watch," Dade ordered, and he took out his phone.

Because of the shrill security alarms, she couldn't hear much of what Dade was saying, but he'd no doubt called Grayson because she could see him on the phone, as well. She hoped they were figuring a way out of this nightmare.

There was movement just to the right of

the smoke, and Kayla spotted the gunman again. He aimed and fired. The bullet flew past her, so close that she could have sworn she felt the heat from it.

Kayla reached out from the tree and fired back. With her shaky aim, she doubted she had hit anything other than the burning house, but she wanted to keep the shooter at bay. She didn't want to give him a chance to get closer to the ditch.

Dade slapped his phone shut and shoved it back into his jeans pocket. "We need to keep the gunman busy. Mason and the fire department are on the way, but Grayson's not going to wait for him. He'll go ahead and get Connie and Robbie away from here."

Kayla couldn't even manage a *thank God,* but she was beyond thankful that Grayson had put her baby first. She wanted Robbie far away from the bullets. Still, how did Grayson plan to get them into his truck?

"Stay here," Dade told her. That was it, all the warning she got before he dived out from cover and behind the adjacent tree.

The gunman fired at Dade.

Of course.

And she realized this was exactly what Dade wanted their attacker to do.

Dade moved again, jumping the narrow space between cover and the next tree. From the corner of her eye, she saw Grayson's truck speed forward.

The gunman saw it, too.

And he turned in that direction.

Kayla forced her hand to steady, and she fired a shot. The gunman jerked back as if he'd been shot and disappeared into the smoke again.

Grayson came to a stop, and the passenger's door flew open. Connie must have figured out quickly what was going on because it was only a few seconds before she came out of the ditch. With Robbie clutched close to her, she jumped into the truck. The moment the door was closed, Grayson sped away.

Kayla was so relieved that tears sprang to her eyes, but she blinked them back. Yes, her baby was safe, but now Dade and she had to finish this.

She glanced over at Dade when he motioned toward the backyard. At first Kayla didn't see the gunman, but she picked through the smoke and outbuildings and finally spotted him. He was crouched behind a large metal container in the corral area.

"You stay here," Dade mouthed. "I'll circle around behind him."

Kayla wanted to scream *no!*, that he should wait for backup, but Dade had already turned his back on her and was darting to another tree. He continued that way until he reached the last tree, and then he dropped to the ground.

When her lungs began to ache, Kayla forced herself to breathe, even though the air was clogged with smoke. She kept her wrist braced to help with the jitters, and she prayed her aim would be good enough to help Dade and keep him alive.

He was risking so much for Robbie and for her.

And the risks continued.

Kayla's heart started beating like crazy when she lost sight of Dade. The gunman was still there, lurking behind the container. He wasn't far enough out in the open to give her a clean shot, and she couldn't take one for fear of accidentally hitting Dade.

She spotted more movement. Not from the gunman, but from Dade. He was creeping along the side of the wooden corral fence. Because she could see him, she did something about creating a diversion. Kayla fired a shot just to the left of the container. It worked.

The gunman shifted in that direction.

It wasn't much, but it was enough. Dade vaulted over the fence and raced across the corral. Kayla was terrified and could only watch and wait. If necessary, she could fire another diversion shot.

It wasn't necessary.

Dade made it all the way to the container before the gunman whirled around. Too late. Dade knocked the gun from his hand and jammed his own weapon against the man's head.

Kayla broke into a run toward them, and she kept her gun aimed and ready. Dade made eye contact with her. Just a glance. Just enough to reassure her that this attack had come to an end.

But then she got a good look at the gunman's face.

A face she recognized.

And Kayla realized this wasn't over. No. This was just the beginning.

Chapter 10

Every muscle in Dade's body was primed for a fight. Yeah, Kayla and he had managed to capture the person who'd tried to kill them, but that person wasn't talking.

Danny Flynn, however, was smirking.

Despite the handcuffs and ankle shackles, the SOB *lounged* in the interview room while Carrie and another medic bandaged the graze wound on the top of his left shoulder. It wasn't a serious enough injury for him to go to the hospital. Besides, Dade didn't want this snake out of his sight.

"If this were the old days, I could beat a confession out of him," Mason mumbled. His brother was right behind Kayla and him, and all three of them were glaring at the hired gun who had refused to answer a single question, much less admit his guilt in nearly killing Kayla and Dade.

"I wish I could just slap that stupid smile right off his face," Kayla added, earning as close to an approving nod as Mason ever gave. "He put my baby in danger, and by God, he's going to pay for that."

Dade felt the same way. But Flynn had already lawyered up, and that meant Brennan would probably pay the bill for the attorney who was on his way from San Antonio. Somehow, they had to get Flynn to confess that Brennan had hired him to kill Kayla.

If that's what had really happened.

The pieces all seemed to point in that direction, but there was a niggling doubt in the back of Dade's mind. Maybe that had something to do with the way Carrie kept glancing back at him. Dade didn't trust her, and he was trusting her less and less with each passing second.

Kayla groaned again, and glanced first at Dade's phone, which he held in his hand. Then, she glanced at the dispatcher who was seated behind the front counter.

"Grayson will call as soon as he has Connie and Robbie settled," Dade reminded her.

That didn't soothe her. Nothing short of holding her son would, and Dade couldn't give that to her right now. Grayson hadn't wanted to bring Robbie and Connie back into town where they might be spotted by one of Brennan's cronies or someone who might inadvertently reveal their location. Instead, Grayson had decided to go ahead and establish a new safe house, somewhere, and Dade wouldn't know the location until everything was in place.

Kayla glanced up at him. There was no longer fear in her eyes. Just the anger fueled by what had to be a bad adrenaline crash. "I don't know how much more I can take of this," she whispered, leaning closer so that only Dade would hear.

"I know." And even though he knew it would earn him a glare from Mason, Dade slipped his arm around her and eased her out of the doorway and away from Flynn's line of sight.

But Mason didn't glare. Well, not at Kayla and him anyway. He glared at Flynn.

The medics finished and packed up their equipment. Tommy Watters came out first

and nodded a farewell to them. Tommy was
fresh out of his EMT training, and this was
probably his first gunshot wound. He seemed
in a hurry to get out of there.

Not Carrie, though.

She stopped, snared Dade's gaze. "How did
this joker find you?" Carrie asked as if she
hadn't already considered the possibilities.

"He followed you." And Dade didn't make
it sound like a question. It was not only possible, it was likely that Flynn had followed
either Carrie and Misty or Winston and Alan.

Carrie shook her head but not before send-
ing a venomous glance at Kayla. Probably
because Dade still had his arm around her.

"No one followed me," Carrie insisted. She
looked around as if to see who was listening. "But her sister made some calls when we
were driving out there. Why don't you ask her
about it?" And with that toss under the bus,
Carrie strolled away.

Dade cursed. He would ask Misty all right,
but he hated the concern that created in Kayla's
eyes. She had enough on her plate without sus-
pecting her sister's involvement in these attacks.

"I'll find out where Kayla's sister is,"
Mason volunteered. "And I'll see if I can

come up with something you can use for leverage to get this dirtbag to spill his guts."

The dirtbag was still smirking. If Flynn had any pain whatsoever from his injury, he certainly didn't show it. No fear, either. Probably because he thought his lawyers would be able to wrangle a deal, but there was only one thing that would make Dade deal with Flynn: for Flynn to hand them Brennan on a silver platter.

Kayla caught onto Dade's arm when he started to move around her and go into the interrogation room. "Can you call Grayson before you question Flynn?" she asked.

Dade didn't have to debate this, even though he knew Grayson was no doubt busy. Still, Kayla had to have some reassurance. It'd been nearly two hours since Grayson had driven off with Connie and Robbie.

Dade shut the door between Flynn and them and pressed in Grayson's number on his cell. His brother answered on the first ring, and Kayla moved closer so she could hear.

"Everything's okay," Grayson assured him before Dade could even speak. "I have Connie and the baby at a safe location."

"Where?" Kayla immediately asked.

But Grayson didn't give her an immediate

answer. He hesitated big-time. "I'd rather not say. We obviously have some kind of breach in security. Maybe a leak in communication, and until I'm sure it's safe, I don't want to tell anyone where we are."

Tears sprang to Kayla's eyes. "But I need to see my baby."

"And you will," Grayson answered. "Just give me a few more hours to make sure I've made things as safe for Robbie as I can."

"How can you do that?" Kayla asked. Her voice was trembling now, and she was on the verge of a full-fledged cry.

"Nate is on his way there to the sheriff's building so he can run a bug sweep. I want to make sure Brennan or one of his henchmen didn't plant some kind of listening or tracking device. Then, Nate will interview all four people who went to that safe house because one of them could have leaked your location."

So that meant Winston, Alan, Carrie and Misty would all be brought back in. Good. Dade was to the point where he didn't trust any of them.

"When I'm sure it's safe to do so, I'll arrange to have Dade bring you here. Okay?" Grayson asked.

It took her several seconds to agree.

"Okay." It certainly wasn't the arrangement she wanted, but it would have to do. Robbie's safety came first.

"I'll have Nate call you when he's done," Dade told his brother, and he ended the call. He turned to Kayla. "Why don't you wait in my office while I talk to Flynn?"

Her breath rushed out with her words. "I don't want to. I want to hear what he has to say."

Dade couldn't have her in the interrogation room with Flynn. He had to follow the rules. Well, the basic ones anyway. Plus, Kayla was on the verge of losing it, and if she went after Flynn and tried to slap that smile off his face, she might get hurt.

"You can watch and listen in the room next door," Dade let her know. "There's a two-way mirror."

Kayla looked as if she might argue, but Dade brushed a kiss on her lips. "I won't be long." And he ushered her into the observation room.

Because the camera was already positioned near the two-way mirror to record Flynn's interview in the other room, Dade went ahead and turned it on to start the recording. He was about to go back to Flynn when he saw Mason making his way back toward him.

"I just got off the phone with Nate's contact at SAPD," Mason explained. "Flynn has a teenaged son that he calls Little Dan. Apparently, he's the apple of Flynn's wormy little eyes. The kid just turned sixteen and has a juvenile record. When he was in lockup last year, Little Dan lost it. Had some kind of panic attack because he's claustrophobic. My advice is play dirty with that bit of info and see where it gets you."

Dade would. Flynn certainly hadn't minded the dirty play when he fired those shots around Robbie and Kayla, so Dade would give him a little of his own medicine.

Flynn sat, waiting. Oh, yeah. He was a pro at this. Dade knew the man was thirty-six and had been arrested four times for assault and breaking-and-entering. However, there had been no arrests in the past two years since he'd been on Charles Brennan's payroll.

"You're wasting your time," Flynn volunteered the moment Dade stepped inside. His smile widened, revealing tobacco-stained, chipped teeth. With the yellowy gray in his dark hair, Flynn looked much older than his years. "I'm not saying anything to you."

Dade read him his rights. Then, he swiveled the empty metal chair around and sat in it so that he could casually drape his arms over the back. He wanted to look as laid-back as Flynn, even though inside him there was a bad storm brewing. Dade really wanted to beat this guy senseless for trying to kill Kayla.

"You don't need to say anything," Dade said. "I'll just keep you company until your lawyer arrives. Then we'll process you and put you in a holding cell." Dade forced a smile. "Look at you. So relaxed. Not bothered at all by any of this. Nothing like your son. He's really making a fuss over at SAPD."

Flynn's smirk evaporated. "What the hell does that mean?"

Dade shrugged. Paused long enough to get Flynn to squirm. "SAPD picked up Little Dan about a half hour ago."

Flynn would have come across the table if it hadn't been for the shackles tethering him to the chair. "You got no right to touch my boy."

"Oh, yeah? Well, SAPD disagrees. An eyewitness tied Little Dan to the shootings." Dade shook his head, feigning concern. "Accessory to attempted murder. And from what

I hear from my brother over at SAPD, they're going to charge your *boy* as an adult."

Flynn made a feral sound and violently shook the chains. "I need to call him *now*."

Another headshake. "You got one phone call, and you made it to your lawyer."

"You can't do this." Flynn's jaw was iron stiff. "Little Dan can't stand to be penned up. He gets these fits, and he'll need his meds. He'll go crazy without 'em."

Dade made a sound of understanding. "Yeah, that probably explains why he tried to call you when he was picked up. But, of course, we have your phone in evidence, so his call went to voice mail. Too bad. I heard the officers had to get rough with him to put him in that cell."

Flynn opened his mouth again as if to make that animal sound, but then he squeezed his eyes shut and groaned. "He had nothing to do with this. Let him go."

"Can't do that. Attempted murder of a baby, a witness in protective custody and a deputy sheriff. Those charges aren't just going away."

Flynn's breath came out in short angry spurts, and the veins popped out on his forehead. The seconds crawled by, and Dade hoped Flynn would say something, anything, before the lawyer waltzed in and uncovered Dade's lie. The lie would hold up in court because cops were allowed to give false information during interrogation. However, the lawyer would no doubt advise Flynn to stay quiet.

"What do you want to hear?" Flynn growled.

"The truth, of course." And Dade waited and did some praying.

"My son had nothing to do with this," Flynn repeated. "So as soon as I've had my say, you'll make a call to get him released. Deal?"

Despite the time eating away at him, Dade pretended to think about that. "If you convince me that Little Dan is innocent, then I'll make that call."

Flynn's dirt-brown eyes narrowed. His mouth shook because his teeth were clenched so tight, but he finally nodded. "Charles Brennan hired me and Raymond Salvetti to scare his daughter-in-law. To do that, we had to find her, so we had someone watching her sister. I followed her out to the house where you and Kayla were hiding out."

Oh, that didn't help Dade's anger to hear it aloud, and he wondered how Kayla was doing with this. Maybe she would come bursting into the room.

"Scare?" Dade challenged. "You fired shots at her. You tried to kill her."

"No," Flynn quickly disagreed. "The orders were to scare her, but Salvetti got trigger-happy and fired into the estate. That was his doing, not mine. Hell, I could have blown up the house today with her in it, but those weren't my orders. I was just supposed to grab that baby and get out of there fast."

It took a moment for Dade to tamp down the emotion, the anger. Nope, it was rage. He hated this slimy piece of filth in front of him.

"Why take the baby?" Even though Dade was sure he already knew the answer, he wanted this on tape.

Flynn dragged in a weary breath. "For leverage. Brennan figured his daughter-in-law would do anything, including keeping her mouth shut, to get that kid back."

Yeah, that was what Dade had expected, but he hadn't expected for it to feel as if someone had slugged him. Robbie and Kayla could have been hurt or killed.

"Why did Salvetti call Kayla's cell?" Dade pressed.

"To make her look suspicious." Flynn

cursed. "But Salvetti wasn't too bright because he wasn't supposed to call me."

Well, that explained that, and Dade believed the man was telling the truth. "What about Kayla's sister? Was that call to set her up, too?"

"I don't know." Another quick answer. "Salvetti was taking his orders directly from Brennan, not me. So, I don't know why he'd call anyone. Now, it's your turn. Phone your cop buddies and get my boy out of lockup."

Dade met him eye to eye. "If I do that, you'll just recant all of this later. What I want is proof that links you and Salvetti to Brennan."

Flynn looked up at the ceiling as if seeking divine intervention. Dade just waited him out, hoping the lawyer or Kayla wouldn't come barging in.

"There's something that ties Salvetti to a crime. If you dig hard enough, I'm betting you can connect the dots from Salvetti to Brennan. But if I tell you, you've got to promise witness protection for me and my boy."

"You know I can't make a promise like that, but I'll see what I can do." And Dade would. Because as much as Dade despised Flynn, he despised Brennan more and wanted to put him away for life. "What proof do you have?"

Flynn swallowed hard. "There's a wall safe in my house in San Antonio. Inside there's a gun with Salvetti's fingerprints. That gun was used in a murder."

Dade heard the voices in the front part of the building and figured the lawyer had arrived. "Connect the dots for me," Dade insisted. "What does this gun and murder have to do with Brennan?"

Flynn leaned closer. "Salvetti has worked for Brennan a long time. Longer than me. And he was working for Brennan when this murder happened. My advice? Dig into it. Now, *please* call SAPD."

Dade heard the hurried footsteps coming down the hall. Two sets. One belonged to Mason, he soon learned, and the others belonged to Darcy Burkhart, an attorney who had recently moved to Silver Creek. But Darcy was no stranger to Dade. No. She had been one of Brennan's attorneys during the initial investigation.

"This interview is over," the petite brunette said. She was a good foot shorter than Mason who loomed over her, but she still managed to have an air of authority. "I need to consult with my client."

Dade got to his feet. "Your client just confessed to an assortment of felonies."

Darcy stayed calm but fired a nasty glance at Flynn. "I need to speak to him *alone.*"

Dade nodded and used the remote device on the wall to turn off the video recorder as he was required to do. Client-attorney privilege. But Dade thought he might already have what he needed without any additional statement from Flynn.

"Make that call," Flynn shouted out to him as Dade headed for the door.

"I will," Dade lied.

He stepped out into the hall with Mason. The lawyer went in, and Dade waited until she'd shut the door before he said anything.

"We'll need a search warrant for Flynn's safe," Dade instructed. "And we need Brennan back in custody."

"It's already in the works," Mason assured him. "SAPD will pick up Brennan, and they'll execute the search warrant the moment they have it in their hands. You think this will link us to Brennan?"

"I hope so." And Dade hated that he sounded so pessimistic, especially when he realized that Kayla was right behind Mason and hanging on his every word.

"Flynn did confess that Charles hired him," Kayla said.

"Yeah." And that would get Brennan back in custody. Temporarily anyway.

Because she looked ready to fall flat on her face, Dade caught onto her arm and led her down the hall toward his office. "This Darcy Burkhart is a tough attorney," Dade let Kayla know. "She could somehow get it all thrown out. That's why it's important for us to connect this so-called gun to a murder and then to Brennan. That's physical evidence and could be a helluva lot better than just a confession from a man with a criminal record."

"So-called?" she repeated. "You think Flynn lied about that?"

Oh, man. He hated to see her hopes smashed like this.

Dade took her into his office, made her sit in the chair across from his desk. He wished he could give her a shot of whiskey from the bottle he kept in his bottom drawer, but she would need a clear head because she still had to make a statement about the shooting. Instead, he handed her a bottle of water that he'd taken from the small fridge behind his desk.

"I'm sorry," Kayla mumbled. She drank the water as if it were a cure for what ailed her, gulping it down so fast that it watered her eyes. Or maybe that was just more tears on the way.

Dade wanted to pull her into his arms for a long hug. He wanted her to lean on him. But that would be a dangerous mix right now because of the attraction. He settled for skimming his fingers down her arm.

"Everything new we learn just seems to complicate things," she mumbled.

Yeah, it did. Dade would have preferred Flynn to give a clear, no-strings-attached confession, but instead he'd added this mystery gun to the mix. It might be critical, and it might be a smokescreen. But someone had to investigate it. That tied up manpower and resources when all those resources should be focused on picking up Brennan and canceling his bond.

Dade moved some things off the corner of his desk so he could sit. Not exactly touching Kayla but close enough. But Dade didn't watch where he was sliding a stack of folders, and they bumped into the framed photo, knocking it over.

Kayla reached out and picked it up. She

started to put it back, but she froze, staring at the picture.

"It's my maternal grandfather, Sheriff Chet McLaurin." The shot had been taken outside a brand-spanking-new sheriff's office. Chet was smiling that good-ol'-boy half smile of his with his white Stetson slung low on his weathered face. "He was a legend around here before he was killed."

"Killed?" she said under her breath. Kayla continued to study the photo.

"Yeah. He was shot twenty years ago while investigating a robbery. His killer was never identified or caught." And after all these years, that sliced right through his heart. His brothers', too. In fact, it's the reason all the Rylands had gone into law enforcement. A case they couldn't solve.

A wound that couldn't be healed.

"I've seen this photo," she said, tapping it.

Surprised, Dade took it from her and had another look, even though he knew every detail. "There's one in Grayson's office."

She shook her head. "No, I saw it in Charles's office."

"What?" And Dade couldn't ask it fast enough. "What was Brennan doing with that picture?"

"I don't know." She had more water and licked her lips. "About eighteen months ago, I was sneaking around in his files. Looking for anything I could use to get Preston and him arrested. I knew that was the only way I could get out of…my situation. I'd just learned I was pregnant, and I was looking for a way to get out."

Dade felt it again. That jolt of hatred for the Brennan men who'd made Kayla's life hell.

"I remember the picture because it seemed out of place. I mean, there were other photos. Some mug shots. Some taken from a camera with a long-range lens. And then there was this one of the Silver Creek Sheriff's office. I looked at it a long time, trying to figure out why Charles had it."

Dade did the same now. He tried to see it with a fresh eye. His father was in the shot. His mother dressed in her Sunday best. Him, and all his brothers.

"Who's that?" Kayla asked, tapping the image of the person standing next to him.

"My brother Gage." Dade didn't want to feel the resentment for his younger sibling, but he did. "He left home not long after high school and didn't come back." Gage had run out on the family. Just like their father. "He joined the CIA and was killed on a deep-cover assignment."

"Oh, I'm so sorry," Kayla said softly.

Dade shrugged. "Thanks," he mumbled and got his mind off Gage and back on the picture taken all those years ago.

Next to Gage was Mel, the current deputy, who was then just starting her rookie year. Two deputies, long since retired. The then mayor, Ford Herrington, who was now a state senator. And then Dade's attention landed on the man at the far right of the happy group.

Winston Calhoun.

He was the assistant D.A. back then and had every right to be in the photo. After all, it was the grand opening of the Silver Creek law-enforcement facility. But because of Dade's recent suspicions about Winston, his presence in the photo seemed a little menacing.

"Where are the files that had this photo?" Dade asked.

"In the storage room off Charles's office. But it's no longer there," she quickly added. "I went back about a week later to see if I could find anything, and all the files were gone. I'm pretty sure Charles figured out I'd been snooping in there."

Dade didn't doubt it. Heck, Brennan probably had surveillance and knew what Kayla had done. It sickened him to think that the only reason Brennan had let her live was because she was carrying his grandchild.

The picture probably wasn't enough to get an additional search warrant for Brennan's place, but Dade would question the man about it when SAPD took him back into custody.

Which hopefully had already happened.

He reached for his phone to find out the status of that, but it buzzed before he could make the call.

"It's me," Mason greeted in his usual growl. "Brace yourself, little brother, because we got a problem. A big one. And the problem's name is none other than Misty Wallace."

Chapter 11

"What's wrong?" Kayla asked the second Dade got off the phone.

His mouth went tight, and he squeezed his eyes shut for a moment before he answered. "It's Misty," he finally said. "Grayson had flagged her bank account. It's routine when monitoring a suspect who might try to flee."

Kayla was about to argue that *suspect* label, but Dade's expression had her holding her tongue and waiting.

"About twenty minutes ago, Misty cleaned out her account. A detective at SAPD immediately tried to call her, but she didn't answer her cell. So, the detective called her apartment. Misty's roommate answered and told him that Misty had packed up and left." Dade paused. "Kayla, she stole her roommate's handgun."

Oh, mercy. Not this. Not now. What the heck was Misty thinking? This would only make her look guiltier. If that was possible.

"SAPD is looking for her," Dade added.

Of course they would, and then they would drag her back in for questioning. Kayla didn't know which she feared most—that her sister was in danger or that Misty was running because she'd had some part in the two attacks.

Kayla's breath broke before she could choke back the sound, and just like that, Dade was there, gathering her into his arms.

"She's my sister," Kayla managed to say. And that seemed to be enough explanation because Dade only made a sympathetic sound of agreement. "I want her safe. I don't want her out there running around with a gun."

Dade nodded. "We'll find her."

The fear must have flashed through her eyes because Dade shook his head. "Don't go there," he insisted. "We'll find her and *talk* to her. That's all."

"Please," she begged. "Tell them not to shoot her."

"No need to tell them that because the cops know she's scared and on the run. They're trained to handle situations like this, Kayla."

His voice was so calm, so reassuring, and Kayla believed him because the alternative was too hard to accept.

"It'll be okay," he promised.

Dade brushed a kiss on her temple and pulled back so they were eye to eye. That was always a dangerous stance for them because it also meant they were close to being mouth to mouth.

"I can't believe this is happening," Kayla whispered. That included Misty, the attacks and, yes, even this bizarre attraction to Dade. "I'm terrified for my sister. And I miss Robbie so much. It breaks my heart to know that he's in danger. He's just a baby."

"Yeah." He used the pad of his thumb to swipe a strand of hair away from her face.

Like everything else, the embrace, the temple kiss, the simple touch—all those things seemed far too intimate. Ditto for the way Dade dipped his head. Kayla braced herself for a bone-melting kiss, but with Dade's mouth and breath closing in on her, he only shook his head.

"Let me call Grayson and see how close

he is to securing things with the new safe house." Dade took out his cell, pressed in some numbers and then put the call on Speaker. "Grayson, it's me," he said when his brother answered.

"Everything is okay," he immediately said. "I have two Texas Rangers en route, and once they're here, I can head out to pick up some supplies. Then we can make arrangements to bring Kayla out here."

She heard what Grayson said, but it was hard to concentrate because in the background she also heard her son. Robbie was laughing.

"I need to say hello to him," Kayla insisted.

Grayson didn't argue, and soon the sound of Robbie's laughter got closer and closer.

"Hi, Robbie. It's Mommy." Kayla tried to keep the fear out of her voice. Not easy to do. But she obviously succeeded because Robbie squealed with delight.

"He's being a really good boy," Connie let her know.

That put a lump in her throat. "Tell him I love him and that I'll see him soon." Kayla moved away from the phone so that Robbie wouldn't hear her cry.

Dade talked with his brother a while longer, and judging from the conversation, they were working out how she would be transported from town and out to the new safe house. Of course, she would have to be back in Silver Creek to testify.

If Charles didn't get another trial delay, that is.

"You okay?" Dade asked when he ended the call. He slipped his phone in his pocket and pulled her into his arms.

"No." Kayla didn't even try to lie to Dade. Besides, he could see her tears. He kissed one of them off her cheek.

"Kids are tough," he told her. "Robbie probably thinks this is some kind of adventure. He's safe, and right now that's all that matters."

Dade was right. Thanks to Grayson and him, they had her son out of danger. And she, too, was safe in Dade's arms.

"I keep ending up here," she whispered.

The corner of his mouth lifted. "Yeah. Eventually, we'll have to do something about that." But it didn't sound as if he intended for that *something* to include staying away from her.

Just the opposite.

Dade lowered his head. Leaned in—

Just as there was a knock at the door. They flew apart, but not before their visitor got a good look at their near lip-lock.

"Nate," Dade greeted his twin.

Nate nodded, but there was no greeting in his eyes or the rest of his body. He obviously didn't approve of what he'd walked in on. And why would he? Nate still lumped her in the same category as Preston and Charles.

"We located Brennan," Nate explained, sounding all-cop. "A Texas Ranger is escorting him here."

Funny, when Kayla had seen Nate on the computer screen during Misty's interview, he'd looked calm and in charge, but in person she could see the nerves right there at the surface. Nate had that Ryland intensity in spades.

"His lawyer has filed a motion to throw out Flynn's confession," Nate added.

Dade cursed. "On what grounds?"

"Ms. Burkhart claims that Flynn isn't mentally stable, that he's had several stints in psychiatric facilities, and that when you interrogated him, he was in need of his medication. She also says you exacerbated Flynn's condition by lying to him about his son."

Kayla wanted to curse, as well. "Please tell me he's not going to walk," she begged. "The man tried to kill us, and he put my baby in grave danger."

Something went through Nate's ice-gray eyes. Sympathy maybe because he, too, was a parent. "I'll do everything humanly possible to keep him behind bars." Nate wearily scrubbed his hand over his face. A gesture that reminded her of Dade. They weren't identical, but they were alike in so many ways.

"What about the gun Flynn mentioned?" Dade asked. "Is the lawyer trying to kill the warrant?"

"She wasn't fast enough." Nate didn't smile exactly, but there was some relief in his expression. "SAPD already has it, and officers are headed over to Flynn's place now. The warrant allows them to search only the safe, though, so let's hope Flynn wasn't lying."

Yes, and while they were hoping, Kayla added that maybe the gun could be used to put Flynn and Charles behind bars for the rest of their lives.

"Is this lawyer working to keep Charles out on bond?" Kayla asked.

"Probably," Nate admitted. "But until the question of Flynn's sanity is decided, we can act in good faith and hold Brennan. Of course, with his connections he might be able to find a judge who'll speed through the sanity decision."

So, they might not have much time.

"I'd like to be there when you interrogate Charles," Kayla insisted. "Maybe I can rile him enough that he'll admit to something wrong."

Nate shook his head and moved back into the hall. "Can't do that. For one thing, Darcy Burkhart won't allow it." He said the attorney's name like the worst of profanity.

Dade stepped out, as well, and when Kayla looked into the hall, she saw why.

Charles was there.

"We have to follow the rules to a tee," Nate said to her, his voice a whisper now. "I don't want to give Brennan a chance at a free pass." But then Nate stepped aside. "However, there is no law against you speaking to your former father-in-law if you happened to run into him. Like now, for instance."

Kayla nodded. "Thank you." It was a concession that Nate didn't have to allow her. Now, she only hoped she could do something with it.

She maneuvered around Dade and Nate and started up the hall. There was a Texas Ranger on Charles's right side, and he stopped when Charles did. Charles had the gall to smile at her.

"Kayla, pretty as a picture," he purred.

"I was nearly a dead picture. Someone tried to kill me again." She didn't wait for him to deny it. Kayla got closer and leaned in. "You might think you hold the cards, but you don't. If you ever want to see your grandson again, then the hired guns stop now."

Of course, she never intended for Robbie to be in the same vicinity as his grandfather, but her son was the only leverage she had.

His smile faded. "I would never endanger my grandson. And I will see him, one way or another."

"Not if you're behind bars," she fired back. "Your hired gun rolled on you, Charles. Danny Flynn said you sent him to kill me."

The anger flashed across his face. Then, quickly left as the smile had done. "Flynn's a lunatic and a liar. I fired him, you know. Weeks ago. And this is all to get back at me."

She hated that the lies came so easily to him. And hated the sound of the woman's footsteps behind her. Kayla knew it was the attorney, and the woman would soon put an end to this.

"Who helped you put these attacks together?" Kayla demanded. And she prayed he didn't say her sister's name. "Was it Winston Calhoun?"

"This conversation is over," Ms. Burkhart said before she even reached them.

But Kayla didn't give up. "Who was it?" She latched hard onto Charles's arm. "Carrie Collins?"

Still no reaction, so Kayla tried again. "Alan Bowers?"

Now, there was a reaction.

Charles's smile returned.

"Alan," he mumbled. "Now, there's a man with secrets." He leaned in, put his mouth to her ear. "Ask him if he's had anything to drink lately. I think he prefers scotch on the rocks."

Kayla pulled back, shook her head. "What the heck does that mean?"

But Charles didn't get a chance to answer. His attorney wrenched him out of Kayla's grip and marched him down the hall toward the interrogation room. Nate and the Ranger were right behind them.

"What was that about?" Dade asked her.

Kayla had to shake her head again. "I'm not sure. Charles could be trying to put the blame on Alan."

Or maybe that's where the blame should be.

"I'll talk to Alan again," Dade assured her. And he phoned the other deputy, Melissa Garza. Mel, as Dade called her. He asked her to round up the available suspects for another interrogation.

Good, Kayla wanted them questioned again, but this could all be part of the game. No accomplice. Just Charles and his two gunmen: Flynn and Salvetti. One of them dead, and the other was in custody. She wanted to believe that meant things were looking up, but they were dealing with Charles here.

Dade started down the hall, but first he grabbed the picture of his grandfather from his desk. "I'd like to try a little experiment," he explained.

He caught up with the others and ducked into the interrogation room where Mason and Nate were with Charles and his attorney. He handed the picture to Nate and then whispered something that Kayla couldn't hear.

"Let's watch." Dade caught onto her and led her into the room with the two-way mirror.

She watched as Nate set the photo in front of Charles. Nate didn't say a word, even when both Charles and Ms. Burkhart gave him questioning glances.

"What am I supposed to do with this?" Charles asked.

"Look at it," Nate explained. "See if you recognize anyone."

Nate suddenly looked calm and in control. Mason, on the other hand, looked like…himself. As if he preferred to beat a confession out of Charles. Kayla was in Mason's camp right now and wished that could happen.

Charles did pick up the picture, and a thin smile moved over his mouth. "Your grandfather," he said without hesitation. "A complex man."

Because her arm was next to Dade's, she felt him stiffen. Inside the interrogation room, Mason and Nate had similar reactions.

"You knew Chet McLaurin?" Nate asked.

"What does this have to do with my client's current situation?" Ms. Burkhart interrupted.

"Nothing," Charles assured her, and he pushed the photo away.

Dade cursed. "You said those files from his office were missing?"

Kayla nodded. "But I doubt he destroyed them. He probably has storage facilities somewhere."

"When things settle down here, I'll look and see what I can find."

That left Kayla with a sickening feeling. Everything Charles touched turned bad, and she hoped he hadn't had any kind of connection with Dade's grandfather. It was obvious Dade loved Chet McLaurin, and Charles shouldn't be able to hurt the few good childhood memories that Dade and his brothers had about the man.

She remembered the silver concho in her pocket and eased her hand over it. It was silly, but just having that piece of Dade so close to her made her feel better. But it was more than that. She was starting to feel protective of his family. As if she had some right to protect. Some need.

And she couldn't feel that way.

That was a sure path to a broken heart.

Charles's lawyer started the session with some legalese about the validity of Flynn's confession. Nate countered with some legalese of his own, and only then did Kayla remember that Nate had a law degree, as well. Kayla was trying to sort through what they were saying when Deputy Mel appeared in the doorway. She held out the phone for Dade.

"It's SAPD calling about that search warrant," the deputy explained. "I figured you'd want to talk to them."

Dade practically snatched the phone from her hand. "Deputy Dade Ryland."

Kayla moved closer, trying to hear the conversation, but the discussion being piped in from the interrogation room blocked out whatever was being said. Plus, Dade wasn't giving anything away. He was just listening.

"Do that ASAP," Dade instructed, and he ended the call.

"Did they find anything in the safe?" Kayla immediately asked.

"Yeah." Dade turned for the door. "Now, let's see if it's important to this investigation."

That's all Dade said before he turned the camera on and darted out and into the interrogation room next door. His entrance grabbed everyone's attention, and the lawyer was no doubt on the verge of objecting when Dade bracketed his hands on the interrogation table and got right in Charles's face.

"SAPD just executed the search warrant of Danny Flynn's safe." And he waited, the seconds crawling by.

"So?" the lawyer and Charles said in unison.

Dade glanced at his brothers first. "They found a gun. A .38 and a spent bullet."

Kayla couldn't believe it. Flynn had told the truth. Well, about that anyway.

"What do you know about the gun?" Dade demanded.

Charles pulled back his shoulders. His only reaction before he shrugged. "I know nothing about it. And when you test it, as I'm sure you will, you still won't be able to link it to me. Because I didn't have anything to do with that gun or anything else in Flynn's safe."

Dade didn't pull back. "That's because you're a coward. You hire people to do your killing."

The lawyer objected of course. Nate countered that objection, and while they were engaged in verbal banter, Dade and Charles just stared at each other. Except Charles's expression was more of a glare now.

Good.

Dade had managed to hit a nerve and that wasn't easy to do.

Kayla went closer to the tiny speaker mounted on the wall so she wouldn't miss any of the conversation.

"If the gun's not connected to you," Dade said to him, "then why would your disgruntled former employee lead us right to it?"

Charles's glare softened, and the cockiness

returned. "Do you want me to guess why a nutjob would keep a gun and a shell casing in his safe?"

"Sure. Guess." Dade had some cockiness, too.

"I think Flynn was hiding a secret," Charles calmly provided.

"What kind of secret?" Dade demanded over the protest of the attorney.

Charles waved off his lawyer. Then smiled a smile that only he and Satan could have managed.

"Just guessing here, mind you," Charles said, his voice low and calculated, "but I think it's a secret that could bring you Ryland boys to your knees."

Chapter 12

Dade felt numb and in shock. Yeah, it was stupid to put faith in anything Brennan said, but Dade couldn't shake the feeling that in this one instance, Brennan had told the truth.

It's a secret that could bring you Ryland boys to your knees.

Did that gun have something to do with his grandfather's murder? Maybe. And if so, Flynn might have handed them the evidence to solve a two-decades-old crime.

Darcy Burkhart cleared her throat. She didn't groan exactly, but she looked as if that's what she wanted to do. Dade could understand why. Brennan had just said way more than he should have.

"I need to speak privately with my client." Ms. Burkhart glanced at the mirror. *"Privately,"* she emphasized. She stood and motioned for Brennan to do the same. "Is there another room we can use?"

Nate and Mason exchanged glances, and it was Nate who escorted them in the direction of the other interrogation room down the hall.

"I've got calls to return," Mason mumbled and headed out.

Dade took a deep breath so he could go back to the observation room with Kayla, but she came to him. She caught onto him when he stepped in the doorway and hugged him. It seemed natural, and it was far more comforting that it should have been.

"Charles likes to play mind games," Kayla reminded him.

Dade didn't doubt that, but maybe this wasn't a game. "The gun might be connected to my grandfather's murder. We never found the killer or the murder weapon. But there's a bullet that was taken from his body. We can do ballistics to see if this gun killed him."

"When will you know?" she asked.

He shook his head. "I asked that the test be

run ASAP. Nate can give them a shove, so we might know something…soon."

And Dade hoped they could live with the consequences of the truth. Oh, man. This could hurt bad. "In the back of mind, I always wondered if my father had something to do with that murder."

There. He'd said it aloud. A first. Probably all of his brothers had thought it, but it seemed too sick to put into words.

"I'm so sorry, Dade." Like her hug, it was the right thing. It soothed him as much as anything could have. It also reminded him how deep the pain was from the loss of his father and grandfather.

It was a pain he didn't want to feel. But damn, that gun had brought it all back to the surface.

"My father left just days after my grandfather was killed," he heard himself say. "And he and my grandfather weren't the best of friends. Both of them could be hard men, and they clashed."

She eased back. Her eyes met his. "But what motive could your father have had for killing him? And then how would Flynn have gotten the gun?"

"I don't know." He scrubbed his hand over

his face. "I just know that our grandfather's death left a big hole in the family."

Kayla just stood there. Listening. Waiting for him to continue. She was offering him a chance to talk this through, and Dade was surprised, shocked even, that he wanted her to hear it.

"It'll always hurt," Dade explained. "It was like being ripped apart, and then Grayson had to put us all back together again." Dade paused because he had no choice. "Grayson's the father that our real dad should have been. He raised us all. Mason, too. He helped raise us while he built the ranch into one of the best in the state."

"You helped with that," Kayla told him.

Dade shook his head and turned away from her. "I helped with roundups and picking up breed stock. Mason is the reason people respect the ranch. Grayson is the reason they respect the law and the family."

"You're a deputy sheriff," she pointed out.

"Right." Man, this hurt, too, but he thought he'd buried it deep enough. Apparently not. "Nate's a cop superstar at SAPD. And Kade, the youngest, he's made a good name for himself in the FBI. Gage did the same in the CIA before he was killed in the line of duty.

Like I said, I'm ordinary, but that's okay. I've learned to live with that."

Kayla closed the door. Well, actually she slammed it. Then, she caught onto his arm and whirled him around to face her. Dade saw it then. The anger in her eyes.

"You are not ordinary," she insisted. "You saved my life. My son's life. You've bucked up against your family to protect me."

The anger faded, and there was a moment. One scalding moment where Dade thought he was going to kiss her again. Kayla must have felt it, too. That pull deep within her. Because she shook her head and gave a reluctant smile.

"Besides, you're too hot to be ordinary," she said. "Want to hear a schoolgirl-like confession? You're hands-down the hottest guy I've ever kissed. When you walk into a room, Dade, I have to remind myself to breathe."

Dade had to mentally replay that three times before it sank in. He waited for the punch line, waited for Kayla to say she was just kidding. But she didn't. She leaned in and brushed her mouth against his.

When her eyelids fluttered up, and he saw those baby blues, he knew this was no joke. Kayla thought he was hot. So, he kissed her, hard, just the way he'd dreamed of kissing her.

The rap on the door got rid of the cocky smile that Dade was sure was on his face.

The door flew open, and he spotted his brothers. Nate looked hurt and confused. Mason looked ready to rip off their heads, especially Dade's.

"Before you have another, uh, private conversation, you might want to check the recording system. It's on." Nate pointed to the camera and microphone mounted just behind the two-way mirror. The very camera that Dade himself had turned back on before the picture confrontation.

Hell.

Kayla's face turned flame red, and she shifted her position so that her back was to his brothers.

Dade wished he could dig a hole for both of them, but he knew that groveling and looking embarrassed wasn't the way to go.

"Yeah, I kissed her," Dade admitted. "Either of you got a problem with that?"

Nate dodged his gaze, shook his head and walked away. Which meant he did have a problem with it, but he respected Dade too much to say anything.

Mason's mouth tightened as he pushed himself away from the doorjamb he was leaning against. "When you screw up, you don't do it half-assed, do you, little brother?"

No, he tended to go full-blown with it. And in this case, it was a screw-up that he knew he couldn't avoid. Kayla was under his skin, and Dade thought maybe that's exactly what he wanted.

"By the way, three of our suspects were just brought in," Mason let him know. "Winston, Alan and Carrie. Let's just say, they aren't so happy to be here, and because Grayson's not back to ask the questions, that means one of us draws the short straw."

"I'll do it," Dade volunteered. He wanted to do it because each question, and answer, could help get Kayla and Robbie out of danger.

"When is Grayson expected back?" Kayla asked, her voice wavering a little. Yeah, Mason could be intimidating as hell, but Grayson's return meant she could see Robbie.

"Not for a while," Mason told her. "Once the Rangers are in place, Grayson said he still needs to pick up some supplies. Plus, it's getting late, and it won't be a direct drive out to the safe house. That's a long-winded way of saying it might be morning before we can get you out there."

Kayla sighed, obviously disappointed. She was beyond anxious to see her baby, and once Dade finished the interrogations, he needed to call Grayson and see if he could hurry things along. Besides, Dade wanted Kayla at the safe house, too, so she wouldn't be under the same roof with Brennan and the other suspects.

"I'll bring the three in here," Dade told her. "So you can watch and listen. We already know the sound system is working," he grumbled. But he added a smile to that and landed a kiss on her cheek.

"It's SAPD again," Mel said, coming up the hall. She handed Dade the phone. "He says it's important."

Dade took the phone and also took a deep breath. Important could be code-speak for bad news. "Deputy Dade Ryland," he answered.

"This is Captain Shaw Tolbert, SAPD. I'm Nate's boss. We got an immediate match on that spent shell casing retrieved from Flynn's safe."

Oh, man. He was right, code-speak for bad news. "That means the casing must have already been in the system." Which meant it had been used in a crime.

"Yes." And that's all the captain said for several moments. "And your informant, Flynn, was right. Salvetti's prints were on the weapon. I figured it'd be best if I told you, and then you could break the news to Nate."

"Nate?" Dade questioned.

The captain mumbled another "yes." Then, he paused again. "The bullet is a perfect match to the one that killed Nate's wife."

To Kayla it felt as if everything was moving in slow motion and spinning out of control at the same time.

She'd watched from the hall as Dade told his brothers about the bullet. She saw the pain register on their faces—an old wound opened up again—and she felt that same pain deep within her.

The Rylands had suspected all along that Charles had been behind Ellie's murder, and they'd apparently been right.

Well, maybe.

"Only Salvetti's prints were on the gun," Dade explained, relaying what the captain had told him just minutes earlier during their phone conversation. "And there's nothing to indicate it's been tampered with. The prints are clean, in places they should be on a gun, so they haven't been planted. This gun is the real deal."

No one said anything right away. All stood there, obviously trying to absorb the horrible news they'd just learned. "The gun can't be linked to Brennan," Mason concluded, and he punctuated that with some raw profanity.

"Not directly," Dade agreed. "But we all know that Ellie's last assignment as a cop was to investigate one of Brennan's drug-pushing henchmen. And she was killed carrying out that investigation. Captain Tolbert said he was personally going to take another look at the case and see if he can make a strong enough connection between Salvetti and Brennan."

Because Salvetti was dead, that might be harder to do, but there was a bottom line here: Salvetti had been the one to kill Nate's wife, and the man had almost certainly been taking orders from Charles. Now, Nate had the gun that might eventually point to Charles, but Kayla didn't think it was going to make it easier for him to accept his wife's murder.

As if he knew what she was thinking, Nate looked up, snared her attention. "I'm sorry," Kayla said because she didn't know what else to say.

He nodded, mumbled something under his

breath, and much to Kayla's surprise, Nate walked toward her. He closed his eyes a moment, but when he opened them, his attention was focused fully on her.

"I know Brennan is making it hard for you to testify, but please don't back down," Nate told her. "You might be the only person who can get him to pay for what he's done."

"I won't back down," Kayla promised. She repeated it so the others would hear. "One way or another, I'm putting Charles Brennan behind bars. Or better yet, in the grave. I want him on death row."

Mason nodded. So did Nate. Dade lowered his head, shook it, and mumbled something she couldn't hear.

Nate glanced back at his brothers. "We'll keep your son safe, no matter what. You have my word on that." When his eyes started to water, Nate quickly turned and moved away. "I have to get out of here for a while."

No one questioned that, and Kayla totally understood. She hated being this close to Charles, but now she had just one more reason to hate him—he'd hurt Dade and his family by taking the life of one of their own.

Dade glanced around as if trying to figure out where to start. He finally hitched his thumb toward the interrogation room. "I'll start with Winston and Alan," he told Mason. "I'll talk to them together. Why don't you deal with Carrie?"

"I'd rather deal with a PMS-ing diamond-back." Mason's mumble was drenched in sarcasm. "What about Brennan?"

"Let him and his lawyer stew for a while." Dade caught onto Kayla's arm. "You can watch from the observation room while I chat with Winston and Alan."

"Remember to breathe, Kayla," Mason said when she walked past him.

She whirled in his direction, expecting to see Mason's usual scary glare, but the corner of his mouth hitched. It wasn't full-fledged, but it was a smile. He gave a half shrug as if he didn't want to expend too much energy for either gesture.

"I should probably tell you that you could do better than my little brother," Mason added. "But it sounds as if this is out of your control."

It was. She had already fallen hard for Dade, and nothing was going to change that. Unfortunately. That meant there were hard times ahead for her because this relationship with Dade wasn't just complicated. It was a potential powder keg.

Kayla brushed her hand against Mason's arm to thank him. She figured the subtle approach was better with this particular Ryland. He made a sound that could have meant anything and strolled away.

"Let's get something straight," Dade said to her on the trek to the observation room. "You won't take any unnecessary chances when it comes to Brennan. We'll get him behind bars."

"And my testimony will do that," she reminded him.

Dade had the same reaction as he'd had in the hall. A head shake and an under-the-breath mumble. "Just don't do anything stupid."

That didn't sound like his first choice of words for a warning, but Kayla couldn't ask for clarification. That's because Carrie came out of the reception area and walked directly toward them.

"Mason will interview you," Dade let her know.

Of course that earned Kayla a glare. She was tired of this woman's reaction and decided to go petty. Kayla leaned over, brushed a kiss on Dade's mouth. "I'll watch from here." Something he already knew of course, and she stepped into the observation room.

"Do I have to remind you that Brennan and she are family?" Carrie said to Dade.

"No, you don't have to remind me."

And much to Kayla's shock, Dade leaned into the observation room and kissed her right back. He added a delicious little smile that Carrie couldn't see because his back was to the woman. Then, he turned, caught onto Carrie's arm and ushered her down the hall where Mason was waiting for her. However, Dade didn't even make it back to the interrogation room before Darcy Burkhart rounded the corner.

"You have a problem," Darcy announced, zooming in on Dade. She glanced in the room at Winston and Alan. Winston was seated, reading something on his phone. Alan was pacing.

"What now?" Dade asked, sounding as frustrated as Kayla felt.

"I'm requesting a trial delay because there's a conflict of interest." She slapped some papers in Dade's hand. "That's the statement I just took from my client. I've already called the judge and the county D.A. I suggest you bring in the Rangers or some other impartial agency to handle the investigation."

Oh, mercy. Had something truly gone wrong, or was this another legal ploy?

Kayla stepped out in the hall to see if she could get a glimpse of the paper that Dade was reading. But he lifted his finger in a wait-a-minute gesture.

"What the hell is this?" Dade demanded, though he'd only had time to skim the page.

"Ask *him.*" Ms. Burkhart pointed directly at Alan.

Alan sank down in the chair, head dropped into his hands, and he groaned. "I'm sorry," he said.

"Sorry?" Dade demanded. "Is it true? Tell me the hell it's not true." Dade was practically shouting by the time he got to the last word.

"It's true," Alan admitted.

"What's true?" Winston asked, getting to his feet.

Dade handed him the paper, and Kayla held her breath as the D.A.'s eyes skirted across the lines.

The color drained from Winston's face. "Oh, God."

Kayla repeated that and was about to ask

what the heck was going on, but Winston glanced at her, then Dade.

"Does Kayla know?" Winston asked.

"No." And Dade said that with too much regret for this not to be really bad news.

"What is it? What don't I know?" she managed to ask.

But Dade didn't answer. He motioned for Mason who was still in the hall with Carrie. "I need to get Kayla away from this and upstairs. It's late, and she's been through more than enough today."

Mason nodded. "What do you need me to do?"

"Have Mel interview Carrie," Dade instructed. "You need to take Alan's statement. After that, he'll resign as the A.D.A., and then you can arrest him and have both Alan and Brennan moved to the jail. I want both in lockup for the night. Call Nate. He can help with that."

"Arrest Alan?" Kayla repeated, but she was the only one of the four who seemed surprised with Dade's order. "Did he do anything to Robbie? Did he hurt my baby?"

"Nothing like that," Dade assured her.

That didn't ease the knot in her stomach.

"We have to talk," Dade said to her. No longer a shout. Practically a whisper.

He caught onto her hand and started walking.

Chapter 13

Kayla didn't ask Dade what he'd just learned, which meant she no doubt knew this was not going to be news she wanted to hear.

Still, Dade would tell her.

It just wouldn't happen in front of Alan or any of the others. She'd had her heart bared enough today without having to go through a semipublic ordeal of hearing Brennan's latest. And there was no mistaking it.

This would be an ordeal.

With his hand still holding hers, Dade led her up the back stairs to the studio-style apartment. Once it'd been part of the jail, but when a new facility had been built five years ago,

Grayson had converted it to a place where they could crash when the workload was too much for them to go home to the ranch. Basically, it was one massive area with a kitchen, sitting space, desk, bed and bathroom, but for tonight, it would be a safe haven where Kayla could hopefully get some rest.

Well, after she fell apart, that is.

Dade led her inside, locked the door and had her sit on the well-worn leather sofa that had once belonged to his grandfather. In fact, pretty much everything in the room was a family hand-me-down moved from the attic at the ranch.

"Tell me," Kayla said, and there was pure dread in her voice.

First, Dade poured her a shot of whiskey from the stash Mason kept in one of the cabinets. He handed it to her and motioned for her to drink.

She did. Kayla took it in one gulp. "Tell me," she repeated. "Was Alan working for Charles?"

"Not exactly." Dade took a deep breath and sat on the coffee table in front of her so they'd be eye to eye. "Alan committed a crime and covered it up, but Brennan found out what he'd done. Brennan insists he hasn't been blackmailing Alan, but it might take a while to prove if that's true or false."

Kayla swallowed hard. "And the crime? Alan's too young to have murdered your grandfather." She paused. Her eyes widened. "He didn't have something to do with Ellie's death?"

Because she was going to need it, Dade inched closer and pulled her deep into his arms. "According to Brennan, a little over a year ago Alan was drunk, and he was involved in a car accident. He hit and killed your husband, and then he fled the scene."

She pulled in her breath and didn't release it. Kayla held it so long that Dade eased back to make sure she wasn't about to pass out. "Alan killed Preston?"

"Afraid so." He waited for her to cry, but the tears didn't come. "Preston had a security camera in his car that activated during the crash, but when Brennan came upon the scene just minutes after it happened, he took the camera before the cops got there."

"So he knew all along how Preston died." Still no tears. She shook her head. "Honestly, I thought Charles had murdered him. They clashed more often than not, and I figured Charles got fed up and killed him or had him killed. This sounds horrible, but Preston's death was a relief to me. As far as I was concerned, he was no longer my husband. No longer anything to me."

He touched her cheek. "Are you okay?"

"Yes." But then just like that, something flashed through her eyes. "Oh, God. Charles will try to use this to throw out the case against him. That's why he told his attorney about it after all these months."

Dade wished he could disagree with that, but she was right. "Mason and Nate will be all over this. The Texas Rangers, too. Brennan will go to trial."

Now the tears came. "He can't get away with this. He can't."

Dade pulled her back in his arms. "He won't. It's true—the only reason he spilled all of this now was to call Alan's integrity into question."

"And it will," she insisted.

"It might. But I read through the case against Brennan, and I don't remember Alan's name appearing anywhere in the motion documents. This is Winston's case."

And while Dade might have some suspicions about the D.A., he wouldn't borrow trouble. Eventually Brennan had to run out of luck and dirty little secrets that had so far kept him from doing any serious jail time.

Plus, there was something else. "Brennan implicated himself today when he gave that statement to his attorney about Alan. Brennan obstructed justice by removing that camera from his son's car. That's another charge we can tack on to the others, and we can use that to revoke his bond and put his sorry butt back in jail. Well, for tonight anyway."

Kayla groaned softly. "That's something, I guess." She eased back a few inches and faced him again. "You've been good to me through all of this. I won't forget it."

Dade stared at her. "That sounds like some kind of goodbye."

She looked ready to say yes, it was. But Dade wasn't about to accept a goodbye. So, he kissed her. Yeah, it wasn't fair. It was ill-timed. But it was also what he needed. Hopefully it was what Kayla needed, too.

"Remember," he said against her mouth, "I'm the guy that makes you forget to breathe." He meant to make it sound light, but it sure didn't come out that way.

Her eyes came to his again, but there was no humor, no teasing. "That's true. And if you don't think that scares me, think again."

He brushed his mouth against hers. "Fear is the last thing I want you to feel when it comes to me."

"Too late." Her words ended in a kiss. A kiss that melted right through him.

Dade returned the favor. "Funny, you don't sound afraid." She sounded aroused, and looked it, too, with her heavy eyelids and flushed cheeks.

He felt her muscles go slack, and she slipped her hands around the back of his neck. "I'm afraid you might stop," she whispered.

Oh, man.

That did it. He was a goner. He hadn't brought Kayla up here to have sex with her, but that was an invitation he couldn't resist.

Dade could think of at least a dozen reasons to quit doing this. Damn good reasons, too. But he couldn't come up with any reason that was stronger than the simple truth. He was burning alive, and Kayla wasn't just the source of the fire, she was the cure.

"Dade," she said, her voice mostly breath, barely a whisper.

But he heard her loud and clear. "Kayla," he managed to say, even though it seemed too much to have the sound of her name leave his mouth.

"Your arm," she reminded him and eased back a little. "Be careful."

Careful and his arm were the last things on his mind right now. Dade didn't think he could keep this together very long. He'd never been a patient, gentle lover. Never had a partner who was interested in anything but hard and fast. He didn't think that was true of Kayla, though.

Restraint, he reminded himself in the same motion that he reached for her.

His hand slid around the back of her neck, and he dragged her to him. His mouth went straight to hers, and in that one touch, that one breath, he took in her scent and taste.

So much for restraint.

"Sorry," he said, taking her mouth the way he wanted to take the rest of her.

"Sorry for what?" she snapped back and stared at him. Her mouth was already swollen from their kisses. Her face was flushed. And her heavy breathing pushed her breasts against his chest.

The sight of her melted him. "Sorry for not giving you an out, for not seducing you the old-fashioned way."

Dade kissed her again. Too hard. And yet it wasn't hard enough. He pressed against her, snaring her in his arms, and dragging her even tighter against him.

"I don't want an out," she mumbled through the kiss. "Old-fashioned is overrated. And I just want you."

He didn't have much breath left, but that pretty much robbed him of the little bit in his lungs. So did the maneuver she made by brushing her sex against his.

Hell.

The bed wasn't far, just a few yards away, but the desk was closer. Grappling for position, they landed against it, the edge ramming into Dade's lower back.

The kisses got crazy hot. Dade couldn't figure out where he wanted to kiss her most, so he settled for any part of her he could reach. Which wasn't easy. Kayla was doing some crazy kisses, too, and she was trying to rid him of his shirt. Dade helped. He ripped it open.

She made a sound of relief and lowered her head to plant some kisses on his chest. It was torture. Her hot, wet mouth moving over his body as if she knew exactly what turned him on.

And she obviously did.

Because she made it all the way to his

stomach. And lower. Especially *lower*. When she dropped one of those fire kisses on the front of his jeans, Dade figured this was about to get crazier.

He caught onto her, dragging her back up and turning her so that she was pinned against the desk.

"I want you naked now," he guttered out.

Kayla apparently agreed because she started to do battle with her top. Dade did more than battle. He jerked it over her head and discovered a woman with a flimsy lacy bra. It was barely there, but he removed it anyway.

Kayla was beautiful everywhere. Certain that his theory was correct, he shoved down her pants and pulled them off her. Then, her panties.

Yeah. Beautiful everywhere.

He leaned in, slowly, and touched his mouth to the pink heart tattoo on her breast. She sucked in her breath and froze. She had that deer-caught-in-the-headlights look. She was waiting. And Dade made sure the wait was worth it.

He kissed his way down her stomach. Her skin was like silk. And that scent. Not that he needed it, but it pulled him right in. Dade caught onto her right leg and lifted it over his shoulder so he could kiss her exactly the way he wanted. The way she apparently wanted, too, because she gasped. Moaned. And then cursed.

Dade was positive it was a good sign.

So was the fact that she thrust her hips forward and shoved her hand into his hair.

He would have finished her off then and there, with the taste of her burning like fire through him. But Kayla obviously didn't want things to play out this way.

She jerked her leg off his shoulder, and with her hand still in his hair, she yanked him back up. Not gently, either. Nor was she gentle with his zipper. Kayla was a woman on a mission, and she batted Dade's hand away when he tried to help. She got his zipper down and shoved her hands into his shorts. Dade could have sworn a freight train rammed through his head.

Restraint, he reminded himself again.

It was as useless as the last reminder. Kayla freed him from his shorts and wrapped her legs around his waist.

Dade did try to ease into her, but that didn't work, either. She was tight, wet and hot. And she used those long legs to push him deep inside her.

She made a sound. Not a gasp or moan this time. Her breath shuddered, and the sound came from deep within her throat. Dade recognized it. It was something beyond pleasure. It was a sound he would have made himself if he could have figured out how to breathe.

The moment seemed to freeze. They were there, their bodies fused together. Their gazes locked. And maybe it was because of that intimate position, Dade knew exactly what she was thinking.

This felt good.

No. Not just *good*. It felt *way too good*. He'd figured sex with Kayla would be extraordinary, but this was a million steps beyond that.

"We're so screwed," he managed to say.

"Oh, yes," she managed to say right back.

They didn't take the time to weigh the consequences of this beyond-sex moment. The moment unfroze. The heat roared through them.

And they dived at each other.

Dade caught onto her hips. Kayla caught onto his back and his neck, digging her fingers into his skin and completing the thrusts inside her.

He felt her closing in around him. She was so near climax. This was usually the part when he buried his face in his partner's neck and went to that dark primal place where the only thing that mattered was finishing what he'd started. First her, so he could rid his body of this fire that was consuming him.

But he didn't do that this time.

Dade never took his eyes off her, even though his vision was blurred. He knew this would be over too quickly, and he wanted to see every moment. Record every touch, every sensation.

He wasn't disappointed.

And he wondered how many times in life reality lived up to a man's fantasy.

Kayla sure did.

She met each of his thrusts, but her grip went gentle on his neck. Her fingers stilled but not her body. The climax wracked through her and she reached for him, pulling him closer. So he was careful.

Gentle.

And it was that gentle coaxing and that look in her eyes that ended it all for him.

Dade thrust into her one last time and let himself fall.

Right into Kayla's waiting arms.

Chapter 14

If Dade hadn't kept a grip on her, Kayla was certain she would have slid right to the floor.

All in all, that might not be such a bad thing because Dade and she were half-naked, but with the climax high already starting to fade, Kayla knew that sooner or later they would have to talk.

Best not to be naked on the floor when that happened.

She was out of breath again. Felt as if her bones had dissolved to dust, but Dade obviously had a burst of energy. He scooped her up, deposited her on the bed that was only about twenty feet away. He had the good sense to fix his jeans so that at least one of them would be semipresentable if someone knocked on the door.

Kayla got a good look at him while he was dressing. Mercy. No man deserved a body like that. Lanky but with just enough muscles to make him interesting. And then there were the tattoos. A small dragon on his left shoulder blade and a badge on his hip. Appropriate because he was a lawman to the core.

"I know," he mumbled, sounding disgusted with himself. He dropped down on his side next to her. "I'm sorry."

Well, that took care of any shreds of a sexual buzz. Kayla just stared at him until Dade cursed.

"Hell, I'm not sorry for *that*," Dade amended. But that didn't clarify anything until he leaned down and kissed her. "I'm sorry I didn't use a condom."

Oh. Kayla might have cursed too if her throat hadn't snapped shut.

"I'm not on the pill," she was finally able to let him know. Mainly because it'd been a year and a half since she'd had sex. "But I think we'll be okay. It's the wrong time of the month."

She didn't want to get into a discussion

about her irregular cycle. Nor did she want to think about this one-time sex with Dade making her pregnant. Good grief. She wasn't a kid, and even though this need for Dade had consumed her, she still should have remembered to take the simple precaution of using a condom.

He got on the bed with her, slid his arm beneath her neck and drew her closer. Just like that, her thoughts about the unsafe sex faded, and Dade—and his incredible body—took control of her mind.

"For the record, you're not as delicate as you look," he whispered.

"Delicate?" Again, she wasn't sure how to take that. "I hope that didn't disappoint you."

"Nothing about you disappointed me." And yes, there was some frustration in his voice. She understood that. Kayla was frustrated at the strength of all of this. "Besides, I wouldn't be a good fit with delicate. You're more my match."

He dropped a kiss on the top of her breast. Right on her tattoo. He might as well have poured warm wax over her because the heat went through her entire body. A slow hunger that was still there despite what had happened just minutes earlier.

"Why a tattoo?" he asked, kissing her breast again. This time, he used his tongue on her nipple.

It took a moment to form words, and her fingers found their way into his hair. "A way of rebelling."

"With a pink heart?" he mocked.

She dredged up a smile. "My rebellion has a feminine side. I wanted something pretty." And it was impossible to concentrate with his hand trailing down her back. The slow hunger suddenly wasn't so slow.

"You've got *pretty* nailed down." His breath was hot when he blew it over her nipple that he had wet with his mouth.

Kayla's breath broke, and that hunger suddenly became hot, slick and all-consuming. "What are you doing to me?" she begged.

"Post-sex foreplay." He flashed a grin that could have seduced her all by itself. But that wasn't necessary because Dade had other lethal weapons in his arsenal.

Kayla knew this would lead straight to a broken heart, but she pulled him to her anyway. She wanted his mouth. His body. She wanted all of him, all over again.

At first, she thought the buzzing was in her

head, but then Dade cursed and snatched up the phone on the table next to the bed.

"Dade," he snarled.

Kayla, too, wanted to curse at the interruption, but then she forced herself to remember that one floor beneath them in the sheriff's office there was a major investigation going on. One that was a matter of life and death— *hers*.

Dade put his hand over the receiver. "It's Misty. And she says that she has to talk to you now."

Kayla didn't even try to choke back a huff. She wanted to hear from her sister, was worried about her, but Misty's timing wasn't good. Kayla got up, sandwiched the phone between her shoulder and ear so she could dress while she talked.

Dade lifted an eyebrow at that, but he, too, put his shirt back on. Bedtime was over, much too soon, and it hurt to think this might be the one and only time she would get to have Dade.

"I'm here," Kayla said to her sister.

"I've been trying to reach you," Misty fired at her. "When you didn't answer your cell, I called the sheriff's office, and some woman said she'd connect me. Are you really at the sheriff's office?"

"I'm here." And Kayla decided to get straight to business. "Where are you and why did you take all that money from your bank account?"

Misty made a sound. Maybe surprise. Maybe outrage. It was hard to tell. "Someone's following me. I'm afraid Charles or someone is after me."

Kayla was worried for her sister, but she wished she had more energy to deal with this. "Why would Charles have someone follow you?" She reached over and put the call on speaker so Dade could hear the answer.

"I don't know!" Misty practically yelled. "Why does Charles do anything?"

"I could say the same about you," Kayla countered. "Explain why you took the money from your account and the gun from your roommate."

Her sister made another of those sounds. "Because I'm scared. Didn't you hear what I said? Someone's following me. I need to see you. *Now.* And I don't want any of the cops around. I want us to be alone, so we can talk."

Dade shook his head.

Kayla knew he was right. The last thing

she needed was to be out and about to meet with Misty. "We can talk at the Silver Creek sheriff's office," Kayla pointed out.

"No, we can't. The cops think I've done something wrong, and I haven't. Well, not intentionally anyway."

Kayla groaned and sank onto the edge of the bed. She was a hundred-percent certain she wasn't going to like this. "What did you do?" she demanded.

"Nothing!" Misty hesitated after that outburst. "I didn't know it was Charles who bought that painting, okay? I didn't know."

Kayla didn't even bother to choke back a groan. This was not what she wanted to hear.

"When did you find out Charles was the buyer?" Dade asked.

Misty made another sound. This one was definitely from outrage. "He's listening to us? Why would you do that, Kayla? Why would you let him hear a private conversation?"

"Because there's too much at stake for this to be private," Kayla explained. "Now answer Dade's question—when did you learn Charles had bought the painting?"

Her sister took her time answering. "I figured it out a few days ago. Someone called, a man who didn't identify himself. He said he'd bought the painting as a favor and he wanted me to tell him where you were. I didn't know, but when I told him that, he didn't believe me."

Kayla could only shake her head. "The man who called was likely Danny Flynn, who's in custody for attempted murder. Or maybe it was Raymond Salvetti, who's dead."

"Like I said, I don't know because he didn't give me his name," her sister insisted.

"Did you specifically see someone following you?" Dade pressed.

"No, but I can feel it!" Misty snapped. "And I'm done talking to you. Kayla, I have to see you now."

Kayla took a moment, not because she was debating her response—she wasn't—but she wanted to word this as clearly as possible. Even though any wording would cause Misty to pitch a fit. "It's too dangerous for me to meet with you anywhere but here."

Her sister used some raw profanity. "I can't believe you're choosing that cop over me."

Kayla was about to explain this had nothing to do with Dade, or choices, but Misty slammed down the phone.

Dade pulled in a hard breath, took the phone from Kayla and tapped the receiver.

"Mel," he said to the deputy who apparently answered, "did you get a trace on Misty Wallace's location?"

Kayla couldn't hear the answer, but she saw the frustrated look on Dade's face. "All right. Thanks."

"Where is she?" Kayla asked.

"In town. The call came from the hotel at the end of Main Street."

Oh, mercy. Why hadn't Misty just told her that? Maybe because her sister was genuinely worried that Charles or someone else would find her location?

Or maybe Misty had sinister reasons?

"Don't go there yet," Dade said in that I-know-what-you're-thinking tone. He slid his arm around her. "Focus on the good."

The good. Well, she certainly had some of that. Her son was at the top of that list. The fact that he was safe with Dade's brother was another *good.* And then there was Dade. A *good* of a different kind.

The question came to her, and Kayla didn't even try to stop it. "What will happen when this is all over?"

He tipped his head to the bed. Smiled. "More of that, I hope."

Kayla didn't want to smile. But she did. "Your brothers won't approve."

"They're coming around." He brushed his mouth over hers. Instant heat.

"And in the meantime?" Kayla kissed him back.

"We just remember to breathe when one of us walks into a room."

She laughed. Couldn't help herself. "You're never going to let me forget that, are you?"

"Never," he promised.

Kayla felt herself floating and realized Dade was easing her back onto the bed. She would have gone willingly, but the phone buzzed again.

"Misty," she snapped.

Dade growled something much worse but answered the call. "This better be important," he warned the caller.

But it must have been important because Dade went still. He just listened for what had to be a full minute and then finally said, "No. I'll escort Kayla there."

That brought her off the bed. "You're not taking me to see Misty," she challenged.

Dade shook his head. "Brennan's request for another trial delay was denied. The judge wants you at the courthouse in the morning so you can testify."

* * *

Morning had come way too soon for Dade. The night had flown by despite neither Kayla nor him getting much sleep. Both of them had tossed and turned.

And ached.

Well, he'd ached anyway, and he was pretty sure Kayla had done the same.

Despite the great sex they'd had on the desk, his body had kept on burning for her even after Misty's call and the news that Kayla would be testifying soon. But Dade had finally managed to show a little restraint. There were no condoms in the apartment, and he hadn't wanted to leave her alone to go get any. Besides, she had needed rest.

Not sex.

Except somewhere in the night, sex had felt like a need more than sleep. More than common sense. More than anything. Thankfully, Dade had kept his hands off her so they wouldn't have a repeat round of amazing but unsafe sex.

Kayla had started her morning with a breakfast sandwich and coffee that Mason had delivered and a phone call to Robbie. Despite the gloomy cloud of the trial hanging over her, talking to the baby had helped her mood. It'd helped Dade, too, though he felt a little guilty for stealing some of her parenthood pleasure.

Now, Dade finished up some emails and made some calls while Kayla showered and dressed in the bathroom. They had plenty of time to get to the courthouse, almost an hour, and it was just up the street. Still, Dade knew he would breathe easier once he had Kayla in the witness room where she would remain until she testified against Brennan.

"And then what?" he mumbled to himself.

With luck, the trial would end soon. Brennan would be behind bars. And the reason Kayla was in his protective custody would end, as well.

Dade refused to dwell on that. He had to focus on getting Kayla to the courthouse and up on that witness stand. After that, well, he'd deal with all of that later. However, he couldn't dismiss that he had complicated the heck out of their situation by sleeping with her. Not just sex.

But making love to her.

Cuddling with her in bed was not a good way to sort out his feelings for her. It was just another complication.

She stepped out from the bathroom, and

there was complication number three. She looked amazing. So beautiful. And it wasn't the clothes. The gray top and skirt that had been picked up from her estate was pretty much nondescript. The kind of outfit someone would wear to court. It was the woman wearing the clothes that made them look amazing.

Dade mentally cursed.

All this *amazing* junk had to stop. He had to clear his head so he could concentrate on getting Kayla through her testimony. He was doing a decent job with his concentration until she crossed the room and dropped a kiss on his mouth.

"You look like a cop," she muttered.

Dade glanced down at his usual black shirt and jeans with the badge clipped to his belt.

"That's a compliment," Kayla assured him.

Oh. Suddenly he felt *amazing* again, so he gave in to it and kissed her. Not a peck, either. Dade made this one long and hard. When he finally let go of her, they both were smiling big goofy smiles.

Oh, yeah.

This concentration stuff was working well.

"It'll be okay," she assured him. But then Kayla blinked. "It will be okay, right? You didn't get any bad news when you were on the phone?"

"Nothing bad," he assured her. "In fact, some of it is actually good news. Flynn was transported to the county jail last night, and he begged Winston for a deal. Flynn will testify against Brennan in exchange for a reduced sentence."

Her smile wasn't so goofy now. Her nerves were showing. "Because Flynn tried to kill me, I hope it's not a too short sentence."

"It won't be," he promised. And he would make sure of it. "Winston told Brennan's attorney about the deal with Flynn. Let's just say Brennan is not a happy camper."

She blew out a breath of relief, then stared at him. "You're right, that is good news. But does that mean there's bad news, too?"

He made a so-so motion with his hand. "Alan is out of jail on bond," he continued. "But a deputy from a neighboring town is keeping tabs on him."

Her eyes widened. "You think Alan will try to run or something?"

The *or something* hiked up her nerves. "No, Mason said Alan was ready to take his punishment. He'll be charged with intoxicated manslaughter which is a second-degree felony, and we'll also tack on leaving the scene of a crime. There's no way around it. He'll see some jail time, and he'll lose his law license."

Kayla nodded. "I'm betting Charles planned to use Alan to help him get out of this trial."

"No doubt, but it didn't work." He ran his hand down her arm, hoping it would help soothe her.

"And Misty?" she asked. "Any word from her?"

Dade had to shake his head. This fell into the bad news category. "No other calls from Misty. The Rangers traced her call to the hotel, but she wasn't there when they arrived just minutes after she finished talking to us."

Another hitch in the nerves department for Kayla. Her mouth trembled a little. "Once I've testified, I'll see if I can get in touch with her."

Dade didn't try to talk her out of that. He wouldn't have succeeded anyway because, for better or worse, Misty would always be her sister.

Kayla moved away from him and picked up the pants she'd worn the previous day. The ones that Dade had practically ripped off her. She reached into the pocket and retrieved something.

His silver concho.

"For luck," she said, and she slipped it into her bra, probably because she had no pockets in the outfit she was wearing.

Dade couldn't imagine the concho being lucky, but he wasn't about to argue with her. Whatever got her through this morning was fine with him. He only hoped it didn't set off the metal detector in the courthouse. His brothers would have a field day with his trying to explain why Kayla had his concho in her lacy pink bra.

"Ready?" he asked, checking his watch. "Mason should be waiting for us."

"Mason?" she questioned.

"I wanted two of us to escort you to the courthouse." He tried to toss that out there casually, as if going outside a single block was no big deal. But her safety was the biggest deal of all to him, and Dade wanted to take every precaution.

"Thank you," she whispered as they walked out.

They went down the stairs where Mason was waiting for them. He had his shoulder propped against the wall while he read something on his phone.

"A problem?" Dade asked.

"Just ranch business."

Yeah, the ranch ate up a major part of Mason's time, and Dade didn't want to think of how many hours they'd all spend playing catch-up when this was done.

The building was quiet for a change. Grayson was on his way back from the safe house with Robbie and Connie. Mel was at the jail with Brennan and his attorney. That left the other deputy, Luis Lopez, and the dispatcher, Tina Fox, to man the sheriff's office. But hopefully nothing else would go wrong before they had their full staff back in place.

"It's only a block away," Dade let her know. "But we're driving." With Misty unaccounted for and Alan out on bond, he wanted to be careful.

Mason and Dade put her between them and hurried to the cruiser that Mason already had waiting. They didn't waste any time, and as soon as the three of them were inside the vehicle, Dade drove away.

It took him longer to get out of the parking lot and onto Main Street than it did to drive the block. Dade didn't let down his guard, and in fact his guard skyrocketed when he pulled up next to the courthouse and spotted Brennan.

"Charles," Kayla mumbled, obviously spotting him as well.

Brennan was in handcuffs, and Mel was heading to the side entrance of the courthouse. Probably to avoid the photographers and news crew out front.

Dade and Mason got out first, positioning Kayla behind them. Out of Brennan's line of sight. Or rather that was the plan. But Brennan saw her anyway because he came to a dead stop. No smirk or smile today.

Brennan shot them an ice-cold glare.

"Happy with yourself, Kayla?" he called out.

She didn't answer, but Dade hated that she had to be this close to the devil himself. Dade looked back to reassure her, but then he heard Mason.

"Hell," his brother growled, and from the corner of his eye, he saw Mason reach for his gun.

Dade automatically did the same. He drew his gun and took aim.

But it was already too late.

Despite the cuffs, Brennan rammed his

elbow into the deputy's stomach. His motion was seamless. And fast. Too fast for Dade to get off a clean shot.

Brennan grabbed the Glock from Mel's holster and put it to the deputy's head.

Chapter 15

Kayla was too stunned to move and could only stand there and watch in horror at the nightmare happening right in front of her. Charles had finally lost it, and he looked ready to kill the deputy on the spot.

"If anyone moves, she dies!" Charles shouted.

Mel froze, and Dade and Mason stood there with their guns trained on him.

"Stay behind me," Dade whispered to Kayla.

She did, but she hated that once again Dade and his brother and now Mel were taking the ultimate risk to keep her alive.

Charles kept the gun pressed to Mel's head, and he inched back until he was right against the brick exterior wall. He probably did that so no one could sneak up on him and grab the gun, but he had to realize that he couldn't escape.

Or maybe not.

Kayla got a sickening feeling. Was this some kind of calculated escape plan? Maybe he had someone nearby ready to assist.

Kayla's gaze darted around the crowd of people who, like her, had come to a dead stop. No one looked ready to spring to Charles's aid, but that didn't mean he hadn't managed to pay off one or more of them to help him escape.

Or even kill her.

The crowd and the buildings on each side of them essentially meant they were trapped, literally in the parking lot between the two-story courthouse and the town's mortuary. They weren't close enough to either building just to duck inside. Of course, there was the cruiser and a few other vehicles they could take cover behind if it became necessary.

"Drop the gun, Brennan!" Dade ordered.

Now Charles smiled. "Not on your life. Or I should say, not on Kayla's life, because we both know she's the one I want." He dug his gun into the deputy's head. "The cop here is just a poor substitute."

Oh, God. Was he going to try to trade Mel for her? Kayla didn't want the woman hurt, but if she traded positions with the deputy, Kayla figured it would be like signing her own death warrant.

"Mr. Brennan?" his attorney, Darcy Burkhart, called out. She was in the crowd but was making her way toward them. "Stop this, please. And put down the gun."

"Stay back," Mason warned the lawyer, and thankfully she froze. Kayla didn't want Charles to have any excuse to go on a shooting spree.

"What now?" Mason tossed out to Charles. "We just all wait outside until we freeze to death or your hand gets tired?"

The corner of Charles's mouth lifted again. "I like your bedside manner, Deputy. No, we don't wait. Kayla will walk toward me, and I'll let the good cop here go."

Kayla felt everything inside her turn to ice. She couldn't stand there and let Mel die.

"You're not going anywhere," Dade warned Kayla when she took a step forward.

Mason and Dade closed ranks, stepping

closer to each other so that it created a barrier between Charles and her.

"But Mel…" Kayla protested.

"He's not going to kill her," Dade whispered to her from over his shoulder. "Right now, Mel is the only thing stopping him from dying."

Even though the blood was rushing through her, causing her pulse to pound in her head, Kayla forced herself to think that through. Dade was right. Charles was too narcissistic to commit suicide, and that's exactly what he would be doing if he killed Mel.

"Well?" Charles challenged.

"There is no *well*," Dade challenged right back. "You can't escape. The only thing you can do is give Deputy Garza back her gun and then go into the courthouse so we can get on with this trial."

"It's not a trial," Charles argued. "It's a lynch mob. I know what you did—talking that idiot Flynn into telling his lies so he could get a lighter sentence. You should have offered the deal to me, Deputy Ryland, because Flynn has blood on his hands."

Kayla shuddered. Even though she knew Flynn was a criminal, she couldn't imagine anyone dirtier than Charles.

"Thirty seconds," Charles added. "That's all the time you boys have. If Kayla isn't over here by then, I'll start shooting."

That caused a ripple of chatter through the crowd, and even though Kayla didn't want to risk looking back, she heard some of them running. Good, because she was afraid this could turn ugly very fast.

"No deal," Dade answered. "Kayla stays put."

Charles lifted his shoulder. "Then in twenty seconds, I'll kill someone, and I'll keep killing until I have Kayla."

"Get ready to jump behind the cruiser," Dade warned her in a whisper.

But Kayla didn't get ready. She stared at Charles from over Dade's and Mason's shoulders. She had only one thing that she could use to reason with Charles, and it turned her stomach to have to do it.

"Charles, think this through," Kayla called out to him. "Preston is dead, and if you kill me, then Robbie will be an orphan. You'll never get to know him because you'll be on death row. Is that what you want for your only grandchild?"

"Robbie," Charles repeated, and there seemed to be some regret in his voice. "It's unfortunate but necessary. Besides, I have good lawyers, and that death penalty might not even happen. You'd be surprised how many legal loopholes gobs of money can find. In fact, I think I feel an insanity plea coming on."

Kayla's heart dropped. She'd held out a shred of hope that she could reason with him if she used Robbie, but Charles was too far gone to listen to any reason.

"Jump behind the cruiser," Dade ordered her.

"You and Mason, too," she insisted.

But the words had hardly left her mouth when the sounds cracked through the air.

Oh, God.

Charles fired the gun.

Dade turned, hooked his arm around Kayla's waist and dragged her behind the cruiser. Mason went the other direction and ducked behind an SUV.

"Get down!" Dade shouted to the crowd who all thankfully seemed to be scrambling for cover.

He couldn't tell if the bullet had actually hit anyone. There were shouts, screams and the sounds of all hell breaking loose.

Brennan's lawyer was still begging for him to surrender, but Dade was pretty sure that wasn't going to happen. Her client had just attempted murder in front of dozens of witnesses, and Brennan seemed to be in the mode of last resort.

Unfortunately, *last resort* could get someone killed.

Dade peered around the cruiser. Brennan now had his handcuffed wrists looped around Mel's neck, and the gun was aimed outward, toward the dispersing crowd.

And toward Kayla.

Mel looked pale and shaky. Rightfully so. She'd been a deputy for twenty years now and had never faced anything like this.

Behind him, Kayla wasn't looking steady, either. Her mouth was trembling, teeth chattering, breath gusting, and she was praying.

"Grayson can't come driving into this with Robbie and Connie," she mumbled.

"He won't. By now he's already gotten a half-dozen calls and is arranging for backup."

Dade was sure of that, but what they needed was a hostage negotiator. Nate, preferably. This was one of his areas of expertise, and Dade hoped like the devil Nate was nearby or on his way.

"Kayla?" Brennan yelled. And he shouted her name several times in that same mocking tone.

Each shout made her tremble harder, and Dade wished he could slam his fist right into the man's face to shut him up. He was sick of the games Brennan was playing and even sicker of the effect it was having on Kayla.

"You planning to die today, Brennan?" Dade yelled back. He didn't figure for one minute that would put any fear in the man, but he needed to do something, anything, to rattle this SOB.

"Not me. No plans to die," Brennan assured him. "The deputy here probably didn't have plans, either, but that's exactly what will happen if Kayla doesn't get over here. Now!" he shouted at the top of his lungs.

"Oh, God," Kayla mumbled. She inched closer to Dade. "I have to go out there. I can't let him kill Mel."

Dade had to get his jaw unclenched before he could speak. "This isn't up for discussion. You aren't going out there because Brennan will gun you down before you make it to him. Then, he'll use Mel as a human shield to escape. If he manages that, he'll kill her, too, and anyone else he can take out in the process."

Dade glanced at her to make sure that had sunk in. It had. She nodded. And Kayla got a new look in her eyes. "I have to do something."

"Brennan will make a mistake," he assured her. "And when he does, Mason will have him."

Dade tipped his head to his brother who was about ten yards away. Mason wasn't looking back at the crowd. He had his attention nailed to Brennan, and his gun was ready. Thank God Mason had a steady hand and a deadly aim.

"Kayla!" Brennan shouted again. But this time, it wasn't just a shout. Brennan fired another shot, and this one slammed into the cruiser.

Dade cursed and pulled Kayla lower to the ground, but he wasn't sure that was any safer because a bullet could go underneath the car and hit her.

"How many bullets does he have?" Kayla asked.

Too many. Mel's gun was a full-sized 9 mm Glock, and it held seventeen rounds. That meant Brennan had fifteen more chances to try to kill as many of them as possible. But Dade kept that to himself.

"Mason, if you get a shot, take it," Dade shouted, although that order was just for Brennan's benefit. To remind him that any second now he could have bullets flying at him. Mason certainly didn't need permission to take out a would-be killer.

"How many bullets does he have left?" Kayla pressed.

Dade huffed. "Fifteen."

She huffed, too. "We have to do something to make him use up those rounds."

Yeah. Dade's mind was already trying to work that out. He could maybe move Kayla to another vehicle for cover and put the cruiser in gear and send it Brennan's way. Of course, that was a long shot because Brennan might realize the cruiser was driverless and not fire. Then, there was the danger of moving Kayla. He needed her out of this parking lot.

And then Dade saw a possible game changer.

Nate.

His brother was at the end of the morgue and was peering around the corner of the building. Nate wasn't exactly concealed, and

Brennan would no doubt be able to see him if he looked in that direction.

Hell.

He hoped Nate didn't do anything stupid, especially considering his state of mind. After all, it had been only hours since Nate had learned that Brennan was almost certainly the man behind Ellie's murder.

Dade glanced at Mason who was motioning for Nate to get back. Brennan couldn't have seen Mason, either, but something must have alerted him because he turned his head in Nate's direction.

"No!" Kayla shouted, obviously aware of what was happening.

Dade couldn't risk firing a warning shot because it could ricochet and hit someone. But he had to do something before Nate stepped out and offered himself in exchange for Mel. Brennan would only kill him.

"Give me the concho," Dade said to Kayla.

Kayla's eyes widened, but she took it from her bra. The moment that Dade had it in his hand, he tossed it straight toward Brennan.

It worked.

Brennan's attention snapped in the direction of the silver concho when it plinked onto the concrete parking lot. He fired at it.

And then everything went crazy.

Mel must have realized this was her chance to get away because she dropped to the ground, and since Brennan's handcuffed wrists were looped around her neck, she pulled him down with her.

"Stay here. I mean it," Dade warned Kayla, and he rushed out to help Mel.

Nate and Mason did the same, all three of them converging on what was now a fight to save Mel. The deputy had her hands fisted around Brennan's wrist so that he couldn't aim the gun at her.

But that meant the gun was aimed pretty much everywhere else.

Dade ran toward the scuffle and kept his own weapon ready. Mason did the same. They could only watch as Brennan kicked Mel, trying to wrench her hands off his wrist.

A kick to her stomach did the trick.

Mel fell back, gasping for air, and her hands dropped from Brennan's. However, she wasn't completely out of Dade's and Mason's line of fire.

Brennan grabbed at Mel, no doubt to use her again as a human shield, but he blindly fired the gun in Dade and Mason's direction. The bullet went into the air, missing them, but Dade knew once Brennan had control of Mel that the next bullet would almost certainly find a target.

Hopefully not Kayla.

Dade prayed she was still behind the car where he'd told her to stay.

Brennan latched onto Mel's hair, and Dade cursed when he realized he still didn't have a clean shot. He was so focused on finding a solid shot that it stunned him when he heard the sound.

The familiar thick blast.

A bullet.

The shot slammed into the side of Brennan's chest, but it didn't bring him down. Brennan stopped, and his attention zoomed to his left.

To Nate, the man who'd just shot him.

But it was too late for Brennan to duck and take cover. Nate fired a second shot directly into Brennan.

Brennan mumbled something.

Then he dropped to the ground.

Chapter 16

Kayla held her breath and prayed those shots hadn't hit Dade.

She'd obeyed Dade's order to stay put, but she couldn't stay down. Kayla peeked over the cruiser to make sure Dade and everyone else was all right.

So far, so good.

Thank God. Dade, Mason and Nate were all still standing. Mel, too.

But she couldn't say the same for Charles.

He was on the grassy strip by the exterior courthouse wall, and Kayla watched as Mason went to him and put his fingers against Charles's throat. Mason shook his head.

"Is he dead?" Kayla asked, but there wasn't enough sound in her voice for it to carry.

Still, Dade must have heard her because he said something to Mason, turned and hurried toward her. He holstered his gun and pulled her into his arms.

"It's all right," he whispered. "Charles is dead."

"Dead," she repeated. Despite Dade's grip on her, she started to walk toward the body. She had to make sure.

"He's dead, Kayla," Dade tried again.

But Kayla kept going. Of course Dade was plenty strong enough to stop her, but he must have sensed that this was something she needed to do.

As she approached the body, Mason stepped away to go to Nate. Nate didn't look any steadier than Kayla felt. Probably because he'd just had to kill a man. Kayla leaned down and as Mason had done, she put her hand against his neck to feel for a pulse.

Nothing.

But when she drew back her hand, she saw the blood, Charles's blood, on her fingers.

She stared at the blood and braced herself for whatever emotions were about to slam through her. But Kayla was surprised that she felt nothing but relief. Maybe that made her a sick person, but for the first time in years, she felt free, and she could give her son a safe and happy life.

Some of the crowd came forward, as well. Charles's attorney was at the front of the pack and kept mumbling how sorry she was to Nate and Mason. Winston was there, too. But Kayla picked through the people and caught Nate's gaze.

"Thank you," she mouthed.

He nodded, but this had to be a bitter relief for him. He'd finally gotten his wife's killer. However, that wouldn't give him back his wife.

"You don't need to be here," Dade told her, and he would have ushered her out of there that very moment if Kayla hadn't held her ground.

Kayla walked closer to Mel. The deputy was bruised and scraped up, but her physical injuries didn't look serious. "What did Charles say right before he died?"

Mel glanced at Dade as if seeking his permission, but Kayla stepped between them and looked Mel straight in the eyes. "Tell me, please."

For several moments, Kayla didn't think

the deputy would do it, but Mel finally lifted her shoulders. "He said, 'Tell Kayla it's not over.'"

Both Dade and Mason cursed, but it was Dade who got Kayla moving. This time digging in her heels didn't help because Dade scooped her up and carried her to the police cruiser. The moment they were inside, he drove away, leaving the chaos of a crime scene behind them.

"Brennan said that to get in one last jab," Dade insisted.

No doubt, but it made her sick to think that he hated her so much that he wanted her to be tormented even after his death.

"Grayson will be back soon with Robbie and Connie," Dade reminded her.

She nodded, thankful that soon she would be able to hold her baby. But even now, just minutes after Charles's death, she was already thinking, what was next?

Where would she go, and what would she do?

There would be no trial, so there was no need for her to stay in town. Or Silver Creek for that matter. She cringed at the idea of going to her estate because there was probably still blood and shot-out windows from the attack where Salvetti and Flynn had tried to kill her.

Besides, there were no good memories there.

But where?

It surprised her to realize her best memories were those with Robbie and Dade. The oatmeal breakfast in the kitchen at the ranch safe house. The phone conversation Dade had had with Robbie after Grayson had gotten her son to safety. How had her life, and her heart, become so tangled with Dade's that it was hard for her to imagine a future without him?

"Are you okay?" Dade asked her.

"Yes." But they both knew it was a lie. The adrenaline was roaring through her, and the thoughts and images were firing through her head.

Especially the images.

She didn't want to close her eyes and see Charles, or his blood on her hands, but she did, and Kayla wondered when this part of the nightmare would finally go away.

Dade parked behind the sheriff's building and ushered her in. Judging from the deputy and dispatcher's somber faces, they'd already heard the news.

"Grayson needs to talk to you," Tina,

the dispatcher, relayed to Dade. "Nothing's wrong with your baby," she quickly assured Kayla. "He just needs to go over some police business with Dade."

Dade reached for his cell, but then stopped. He glanced down at her hands. "Why don't you go upstairs and wash up? Once Robbie is here, I can take all of you out to the ranch."

Kayla blinked. "The ranch?"

"For some downtime," Dade clarified. "The town will be buzzing with reporters and gawkers for the next couple of days."

Of course. Because this would be big news. It was possible the entire thing had been caught on film by a camera crew and would be replayed over and over on the news channels.

Dade nudged her in the direction of the stairs, and Kayla forced one foot ahead of the other. Each step seemed to take way too much energy, probably because she was in shock, but she would get this blood off her hands.

The apartment was just as Dade and she had left it, and her attention went straight to the bed with the rumpled covers. The place where Dade had made love to her. Or maybe it had just been sex for him. Later, she would sort all of that out, but for now she needed her son. Once she had Robbie in her arms, she didn't intend to let go for a long time.

She made her way to the bathroom and turned the water on full blast in the sink. Kayla grabbed the bar of soap and started to scrub.

The tears came.

They sprang to her eyes so quickly that she didn't have time to try to blink them back. She hated Charles for what he'd done, but she couldn't completely dismiss the waste of a human life. Robbie's blood kin. His grandfather. A man her son would never know.

Kayla stared into the sink as the blood-tinged water and soap suds spiraled down the drain. She reached to turn off the faucet, but she saw something out of the corner of her eye.

A gun.

She got just a glimpse of it before the arm curved around her neck, and the barrel of the gun jammed against her back.

"Like Charles said, it's not over, Kayla," the person growled in her ear.

"Tina said we needed to talk," Dade greeted Grayson when his brother answered.

"You okay?" Grayson immediately asked.

"Yeah." And that was mostly true. Kayla and he had come out of a dangerous situation without a scratch, and that was nothing short of a miracle. Still, it would be a while before he wouldn't think of how close Kayla had come to dying—again.

"How's Kayla?" Grayson continued.

"Shaken up more than she'll admit. Seeing Robbie will help. How long before you get here?"

"About fifteen minutes. I kept Robbie and Connie at the sheriff's house down in Floresville."

No wonder it was taking Grayson so long to get here. Floresville was an hour and a half away from Silver Creek. But it was smart for his brother to take them that far away. As bad as the ordeal with Brennan had been, it would have been much worse if Robbie had been put in danger, too.

"What are you going to do about Kayla?" Grayson wanted to know.

Good question, but Dade didn't have an answer that his brother would like. "I want to keep seeing her," Dade confessed. "Do you have a problem with that?"

"No, and neither will anyone else in the family," Grayson said as gospel. And it would be. Even though they were all adults now, Grayson was still head of the Rylands, and what he said was pretty much a go.

"Thank you," Dade mumbled.

"Don't thank me yet. We've all got some long hours ahead of us to tie up this Brennan mess."

Yeah. And the mess that Alan had left them. "I'll let Kayla know that Robbie will be here soon."

Dade ended the call and hurried toward the stairs. Despite the fact he'd just witnessed a man's death, he was feeling darn good. The green light from Grayson was no doubt responsible for that and so was the woman waiting for him in the apartment. Dade only hoped that Kayla wasn't standing up there trying to figure out how to tell him that it was over between them, that she couldn't stay in Silver Creek any longer.

His good mood faded a bit.

And then it vanished completely when he opened the apartment door and saw Kayla's expression. She was in the doorway of the bathroom, and her face was paper-white.

"What's wrong?" Dade asked, and he went to her so he could pull her into his arms.

But he froze when he saw the gun.

His stomach crashed to the floor, and every muscle in his body went into fight mode. He reached for his weapon.

"Don't!" someone warned. It was the person on the other end of that gun.

It was a woman's voice, and one that Dade instantly recognized.

"Carrie," he spat out. "What the hell do you think you're doing?"

"Tying up loose ends," Carrie calmly answered. "I thought I'd be finished doing that before you got here. Guess not. I really hadn't planned on killing you, too, but you got here a little sooner than I figured. Now, take out your gun using only two fingers and toss it onto the counter. Do anything stupid, and I'll kill her where she stands."

Dade believed her. He didn't know why Carrie was doing this, but there was no hesitation in her voice.

"Your gun," Carrie repeated. "Put it on the counter. Now."

Dade hated to surrender his weapon, but he had no other choice. He couldn't stand there and watch Carrie kill Kayla. So Dade did as this nutjob asked and laid his gun on the counter.

Carrie inched Kayla forward but not too

far. Carrie's back stayed to the bathroom where there were no windows and therefore no way for anyone to sneak up on her. That meant Dade was going to have to figure out how to disarm both Carrie and this situation.

"Brennan is dead," Dade told Carrie.

"Yeah, I saw it happen. When I realized he'd been killed, I sneaked in the back. Tina was busy on the phone and didn't see me so I came up here and waited. I knew you'd have Kayla wash the blood from her hands."

Even though her every word was critical, Dade listened to make sure no one was coming up the stairs. Grayson would be arriving soon, and Dade didn't want Robbie coming into this.

Dade looked past Kayla. Or rather, tried. Hard to do with that look of stark fear on her face. God, she didn't need to go through anything else. But Dade pushed that aside and snagged Carrie's gaze.

"Is this about me? About us?" he asked. "Because if it is, then this isn't the way to win me back."

Carrie laughed, a quick burst of air, but there was no humor in it. "No, it's not about you. Well, maybe just a little. Let's just say I probably wouldn't have taken the job if you hadn't dumped me for her." She gave Kayla a hard jam to the back.

Hell.

"We broke up months ago," Dade reminded her, although he doubted she would listen to reason. After all, Carrie was holding Kayla at gunpoint. "And if this isn't about me, what is it about?"

"Money," Carrie volunteered.

"Charles is paying her off," Kayla provided. She still had some fear in her expression, but now there was anger, too.

"Hard to pay someone off if he's dead." Dade kept his attention fastened to Carrie. Especially her trigger finger. If it tensed, then he was going to have to dive at the women and pray for the best.

"Charles set it up before Nate killed him. One of his offshore lawyers is holding the money for me. All he has to see is Kayla's death certificate, and the cash is mine." Unlike Kayla, there wasn't a shred of emotion in Carrie's voice. All ice. "He sent instructions through one of his employees for me to help him. First, I took Kayla's phone from her car and made it look as if she'd been in touch with Salvetti."

Well, that was one mystery solved, and it

probably had been easy because Carrie had come to the estate in her official role as a paramedic.

"And then Brennan told you to do this?" Dade tipped his head to her gun.

"Yes," Carrie answered. "He said I was to tie up loose ends if he could no longer do it."

"I'm a loose end," Kayla added. Her gaze drifted to the door, and Dade knew she was thinking about Grayson's arrival. This had to end before his brother came up the stairs with Robbie and Connie.

"So Brennan paid you to kill Kayla?" Dade asked. "Why would you agree to do that? Is this really just about the money?"

"The money…and her." Carrie glared at Kayla. "I was in love with Preston, and she took him from me. She didn't care that she broke my heart. Heck, I'll bet she didn't even love him. She just didn't want me to have him."

"I didn't know about you," Kayla insisted. "Preston never even mentioned you."

"Liar!" Carrie practically shouted. "He loved me, and he would have kept loving me if you hadn't gotten in the way. I should have been the one married to him."

"I wish you had been," Kayla mumbled.

Dade remembered the photos of Kayla's battered face and knew that was true. Carrie clearly had no idea of Preston's true nature.

"So, you're going to kill Kayla because Preston dumped you?" Dade pushed. He wasn't sure he'd get a sane answer, but he wanted to hear it anyway.

"Damn right," Carrie spat out. "I should have been Preston's wife, living with him in a fancy house. I should have had all that Brennan money. Not her. Well, now I'll have some of it, and I'll rid the world of this man-stealing witch who got in my way."

Dade couldn't believe the rage he was seeing and hearing, but he had to keep his own rage in check and get Kayla out of this. "How much did Brennan agree to pay you?" Dade asked Carrie. "Because I can match it."

"A million dollars." Now, Carrie smiled. "Is she worth that much to you, Dade?"

"Yes." And in that moment he knew that was completely true. Kayla was worth that and more.

She was worth everything.

And that included dying for her.

Even if he had to trade his life for hers, he was not going to leave Robbie an orphan.

"Yes?" Carrie challenged.

"Yes," Dade repeated. "I'll make the call and have the money sent anywhere you want. Better yet, I'll double Brennan's offer."

Carrie hesitated, and Dade said another prayer that she would jump at the chance for blood money. But then something flashed through her eyes.

Not just anger.

This was one step beyond that.

"You barely know her," Carrie spat out. "And you're willing to give up so much for her? The witch has brainwashed you. Just like she did Preston. Can't you see that?" She cursed, not waiting for his answer. "You've changed, Dade, and not for the better."

Dade disagreed with that. He had changed. He no longer felt like the bad boy of the Ryland clan. He was the man who was going to save Kayla's life.

"The money?" Dade reminded Carrie. "I'm offering you two million dollars." And he adjusted his feet so he would be able to move better.

"No deal," Carrie told him. "I'd rather have Charles's money."

"You mean you'd rather kill Kayla," Dade fired back.

"That, too."

When Carrie smiled, Dade knew he couldn't change her sick mind. Maybe if she thought she had Kayla out of the way, she would stand a chance with him. And maybe she just wanted him to suffer because things hadn't worked out between them.

Dade glanced at Kayla and gave her a look that he hoped she could interpret—brace yourself.

He lowered his head and launched himself forward.

Kayla didn't have time to react.

One moment she was standing with Carrie's gun jammed to her back, and the next moment Dade dived right into them.

All three of them went crashing to the floor.

Something rammed hard into Kayla, maybe it was Carrie's gun, but whatever it was, it knocked the breath right out of her. Not a good time for that to happen because she needed to help Dade get that gun. It wouldn't be long, maybe just seconds, before Grayson walked in with Robbie.

Gasping for air, Kayla managed to roll to the side, and she got a better look at the life-and-death struggle. The three of them were wound together, and her right arm was hooked between Dade and Carrie.

Thankfully, Dade had managed to get his hands on Carrie's arm, and he had a death grip on her. That was the only thing that prevented the woman from aiming the gun. Unfortunately, Carrie's finger was still on the trigger, and she made use of that.

She fired.

The blast echoed through the room and through Kayla.

It was deafening, probably because the gun was so close to her ear. Certainly someone downstairs had heard it and would come up to investigate. Kayla didn't know if that would be good or bad because it would be impossible for anyone to get off a clean shot.

Kayla tried to move away, to untangle herself, but Carrie must have noticed what was going on because the woman kicked Kayla right in the chest. Her breath was already in shreds, and that didn't help. But it did rile her to the core.

She couldn't let Carrie get away with this.

Kayla rammed her elbow into Carrie and used the leverage to force herself out of the mix. But Dade was there in it, his hands still locked around Carrie's wrist.

Another shot slammed into the ceiling.

Even though it didn't come close to Dade or her, Kayla couldn't risk a shot ricocheting off something and hitting Dade.

Frantically, she looked around the room for anything she could use as a weapon. The first thing she spotted was a heavy silver-framed photo of Dade and his brothers. Kayla snatched it from the counter and brought it down, hard, on Carrie's head.

Carrie made a sound of outrage and tried to turn the gun on Kayla.

Dade cursed and held on despite Carrie kicking any and every part of his body that she could reach. She also managed to get off another shot.

"What's going on in there?" Deputy Lopez yelled from the other side of the door.

"It's Carrie," Kayla shouted. She didn't know whether to tell the deputy to come in or stay put.

"To hell with this," Dade snarled, and he rammed his elbow across Carrie's chin.

The woman's head flopped back, but she didn't stop fighting.

Kayla could only watch in horror as Carrie managed to maneuver her body, twisting it, until she broke free of Dade's grip. For just a second. In that second, Dade grabbed at Carrie again, but Carrie's attention was focused only on Kayla.

"You're a dead woman," Carrie threatened. And she brought up the gun.

Just as Dade latched onto it and Carrie's hand.

He bashed both against the floor. But not in time. Carrie pulled the trigger again.

Kayla immediately knew something was wrong. The sound was different this time. Not so much of a blast but a deadly sounding thud. And she knew.

Someone had been shot.

"Dade!" Kayla yelled. She grabbed him by the shoulder and dragged him away from Carrie.

She saw the blood then.

So much blood.

And Kayla felt her heart stop. God, had she lost him? Had Carrie managed to kill Dade?

The timing was horrible, but the only thing that kept going through Kayla's head was that she hadn't gotten the chance to tell him that she loved him.

"Dade," Kayla said through a sob.

He turned his head and caught her gaze. "I'm okay," he assured her.

But Kayla shook her head and stared at the blood.

Dade climbed off Carrie, and in the same motion, he hooked his arm around Kayla to move her away from Carrie. But Kayla still saw the woman.

Lifeless, the front of her green scrubs soaked in blood.

Carrie still had a grip on the gun that she'd fired. And when she fired that last bullet, she'd accidentally shot herself.

"It's over," she heard Dade say.

And he pulled Kayla into his arms.

Chapter 17

"Are you sure this is okay?" Kayla asked—again.

Dade tried to give her a reassuring nod—again. It had only been two hours since Carrie had tried to kill them, and he figured Kayla would need a lot of reassuring until it was nothing but a bad memory. He took Robbie from the infant seat in the back of the cruiser. Robbie flashed Dade a big sloppy grin and babbled some sounds. Happy sounds. Unlike his mom, Robbie had no apprehensions about coming to the Ryland ranch.

"Da da da," Robbie babbled.

Dade knew he was just trying to say his name, but it melted his heart anyway.

"The ranch is big," Kayla commented as she stepped from the front passenger's seat. She looked up at the sprawling two-story red-brick house.

Dade took a moment to try to see the place through Kayla's eyes. Yeah, it was big and getting bigger. Three thousand acres, but Mason was constantly in "buy" mode when it came to adjoining land. And the house, well, it had gone through changes over the years, too.

"Grayson and Eve are having a new wing put on so they'll have more room for their baby," he let them know. He tipped his head to the addition that had already been framed. "Nate and Kimmie live in the left wing with Kimmie's nanny, Grace. I already called and talked to Grace, and she said she'd help out taking care of Robbie."

"That's kind of her," Kayla said softly.

Yeah, and it might become a necessity because Connie had decided that she needed a break. Dade couldn't blame the woman because she'd spent the last couple of days in danger, in hiding and on the run. Before that, she'd been in hiding with Kayla. Hardly the best employment situation.

Kayla's gaze went from the left wing to the porch that extended across the entire front of the main house. Unlike her estate, the ranch was homespun and didn't have a high-end decorator's touch.

"It's really beautiful," Kayla said, looking back at him. She smiled both at Dade and Robbie, but her smile couldn't hide her nerves. "But I probably should have gotten a room at the hotel while my place is being repaired. Especially because I don't think I'll be going back to the estate."

Dade stopped. This was the first he'd heard of this, and Kayla and he had spent the last couple of hours talking.

"Too many bad memories," she added.

He didn't doubt that, but he didn't like that Kayla was making plans that she hadn't talked about. Of course Dade had done the same.

Her attention drifted to the other vehicles in the drive. Mason's truck. Nate's Lexus. Grayson's SUV. "Your brothers are here."

"Yeah." Dade had made certain of that. It was part of the *plan*.

And that led him to his next thought.

This might be a mistake. A huge one. But sooner or later he wanted his family to meet Kayla and Robbie—*really* meet them—not with bullets flying or while neck-deep in an investigation. That investigation was over now. The danger, too. And it was time Kayla faced his brothers under normal circumstances.

Normal.

Finally.

It wasn't perfect, but they were getting there. No more threats to Kayla's life. No more Brennan. No more Carrie. Heck, Kayla had even managed to reconcile with her sister. Over the phone anyway. In a day or two Dade would see about getting them together face-to-face for a little mending time because they now knew that Misty hadn't had a hand in the attempts on Kayla's life.

"Kade, my youngest brother, is at work at the FBI office in San Antonio, but he'll be here later tonight," Dade let her know. "They won't bite," he whispered and nudged her onto the porch.

"Even Mason?" Kayla questioned.

Dade shrugged. "He'll behave." He hoped. With Mason you were never quite sure what you were going to get.

The front door flew open, and a silver-haired woman came rushing out onto the porch. Kayla would have taken a step back if Dade hadn't caught onto her arm to anchor her in place.

"Kayla, Robbie, this is Bessie Watkins, the woman who takes care of us."

"I do at that. I cook, clean and give 'em you-know-what when they need it." Smiling from ear to ear, Bessie went straight to Robbie. "Now here's a handsome little angel."

Robbie approved of the compliment and gave her a grin.

Bessie scooped the baby right out of Dade's arms, kissed him on each cheek and then hugged Kayla. "Welcome to the Double R Ranch."

"Thank you," Kayla managed, but she still didn't sound comfortable.

"The others already had lunch," Bessie let them know. "But if you're hungry, there's plenty of roast beef and pecan pie left. And I'm fixing a big pot of chili for dinner."

Yeah, and Dade could smell it. Walking into the house was always like coming home for Christmas, and he would never take that for granted.

With Robbie cuddled in her arm, Bessie

ushered them inside, past the foyer and into the massive family room. Again, no fancy stuff here. Hardwood floors, leather furniture and a floor-to-ceiling limestone fireplace with some log simmering in the hearth. The only artwork was family portraits and paintings of some of the ranch's prize-winning livestock.

To Kayla it must have been like walking into the lion's den.

There was a basketball game on TV, volume blaring, and Mason, with a beer in his hand, had claimed one of the oversize recliners. Nate was stretched out on the floor while Kimmie, his daughter, arranged little plastic horses on his stomach and chest. Grayson and Eve were on the sofa making out.

Well, kissing anyway.

"Newlyweds," Dade whispered to Kayla, and he cleared his throat so it would get their attention. It did. Everyone stopped, even Kimmie, and stared at Dade and their visitors.

For one bad moment, Dade thought this had been a mistake to spring Kayla on them and vice versa, but then Eve leaped off the sofa and hurried to them. Like Bessie, she gave Kayla a hug. Dade, too.

"Thanks," Dade told Eve, returning the

hug. Eve might have been only his sister-in-law, but he loved her as much as he loved his brothers.

"Kayla and this handsome little angel are staying with us a few days," Bessie let them know.

She sat Robbie on the floor next to Kimmie, and the little girl—God bless her—immediately offered Robbie one of her toy ponies. There was only two months difference in their ages, with Kimmie being slightly older, but they were almost identical in size.

"Mason will get your bags from the car," Bessie insisted. "Won't you, Mason?"

Mason stared at them. And stared. Before he finally grumbled something and climbed out of the recliner.

"I'll help," Nate said, getting off the floor.

"The bags can wait," Dade insisted, and that drew everyone's attention back to him.

He swallowed hard. It was a do-or-die moment. And everything hinged on what happened in the next few minutes.

Dade took a deep breath and turned to Kayla. "I'm in love with you," he blurted out.

Other than the TV, the room went stone-cold silent. Even Robbie and Kimmie quit babbling.

"I didn't know," Dade continued, "until I saw Carrie holding that gun on you."

"Now, that's romantic," Mason snarled.

Dade shot him a scowl. So far, this wasn't going well. He could deal with Mason's snark, but Kayla's mouth was partially open, and she was staring at him.

A dozen things went through his head, none good. She was about to run for the hills. Or laugh. Or tell him that it was the adrenaline crash talking. After all, it'd been only a couple of hours since Carrie had tried to kill her.

Kayla caught onto his arm. "Uh, we should probably talk about this in private."

Dade held his ground. "I considered that, but I figured sooner or later, preferably sooner, I wanted my family to know how I feel about you."

She nodded. Got that deer-caught-in-the-headlights look. And nodded again. "Okay." She scrubbed her hands down the sides of her dress. "I'm in love with you, too."

That hit him like a sack of bricks.

Oh, he'd wanted the words, but he hadn't expected Kayla to admit it without some prompting. He also hadn't expected to feel this way after hearing those words come from her mouth.

Yeah, it was a shocker. His knees were weak. His thoughts spinning a mile a minute. But most of all, Dade was over the moon.

"It's true?" he checked.

"Yes," she verified and cast another uncertain glance at his gob-smacked siblings.

That *yes* was enough for him. Dade put his arm around Kayla's waist and hauled her to him for a kiss. And not just a peck. He wanted this to be a kiss they would remember for the rest of their lives.

He caught the sound of her surprise with his kiss, and he moved into it, letting the taste of her slide right through him. Like hot whiskey. And sex.

Especially the sex.

But he tried to put that on hold for a moment even though the kiss was a reminder that he would like to drag her off to his bed and soon.

Someone cleared their throat—Bessie, he realized. "Why don't I take the little ones to the nursery?"

"In a minute." Dade figured he might as well go for broke. He looked at Bessie, Eve, his brothers and the babies. "I'm going to ask

Kayla to marry me. I just want to make sure nobody has a problem with that."

More stares.

Except for Kayla.

She made another of those happy melting sounds of surprise and launched herself into his arms. Dade realized then that her response was the only one that mattered. And Robbie's, of course, but Dade and the little guy seemed to be on the same page because Robbie clapped his hands and babbled, "Da da da."

The baby was clearly a genius.

"I love you," Dade reminded her.

Kayla kissed him. Again, not a wuss kiss. This one had Mason growling, "Get a room, all right?"

Both Kayla and Dade were smiling when they finally broke the kiss. "And your answer to that marriage proposal?" Dade reminded her.

"Yes." No hesitation whatsoever, although she did cautiously eye the rest of the clan.

There it was again. The feeling that he'd just been hit hard and loved hard all in the same moment. Dade never considered himself a gushy kind of guy, but he suddenly felt like gushing.

"Well, it's about time you got a good woman in your life," Bessie declared. She hugged them both again.

So did Eve. "Welcome to the family," she told first Kayla, then Robbie.

Nate came next, and Dade knew this was a huge concession for his twin. Nate was still reeling from the news of Ellie's killer, but that didn't stop him from pulling Kayla into his arms.

"You'll be good for Dade," Nate whispered to her.

"He'll be good for me," Kayla whispered back.

And Dade hoped like the devil he didn't disgrace himself by getting misty-eyed.

Nate pulled something from his pocket. A silver Double R concho. "I picked it up from the parking lot," Nate explained. And he took Kayla's hand so he could put it in her palm. "I would give it to Dade, but he might throw it away again."

Dade just shook his head. Throwing it away just wasn't working because this was the second time it'd turned up. "Kayla can decide what to do with it," Dade let her know.

Her hand immediately closed around it. "Then, I'll keep it."

Eve pulled her neck chain from beneath her blouse to reveal her own concho. It was a gift Dade had given her for Christmas. "It makes me feel like part of the family."

"You are family," Dade clarified.

Eve smiled, brushed a kiss on his cheek. "Soon Kayla will be family. Robbie, too."

Grayson was waiting right behind Eve, and when she stepped to the side, his big brother was there to give Kayla his own welcoming hug. This was like the Ryland version of a receiving line.

"This family can always use some more females," Grayson teased. "And apparently another wing of living quarters." But his expression turned more serious when his gaze met hers. "Welcome to the family, Kayla."

Oh, man. That put some tears in her eyes. Eve's, too. This was going much better than Dade had expected, but then, this was his family. There was a lot of love in this room.

Then, Mason stepped forward. He didn't snag Kayla in his arms. He just stared at her. And stared.

"You could do better, Kayla," Mason told her. He lifted his shoulder. "But not much."

Coming from Mason, that was a warm fuzzy welcome, and much to Dade's surprise, Kayla leaned in and kissed Mason on the cheek. Dade couldn't be sure, but he thought Mason might have actually blushed. It was hard to tell under those multiple layers of stubble.

"I'll get the bags," Mason said, strolling out. Nate was right behind him.

Eve scooped up Kimmie. Grayson took Robbie. "We'll show Robbie the nursery. It's like a toy store in there."

"And I'll check on dinner," Bessie piped in, following the others out.

Dade knew it was a ploy to give Kayla and him some alone time, and he was thankful for it. He didn't waste even a second before he pulled Kayla to him and kissed her.

"Marry me?" he said against her mouth.

"I've already said yes."

"Yeah, but I wanted to hear it again."

Kayla smiled, and he caught that smile with another kiss. "Yes," she repeated. But then she pulled back, blinked. "Are you sure about this?"

He didn't blink, but he did frown. "You're not sure?"

"No, I'm positive. I love you. I *really* love you. But I have so much baggage with a bad marriage under my belt."

"Then it's time you had a good marriage. To me," he clarified, causing her to smile. "Because I *really* love you, too."

But again, her smile faded. Because there was nothing she could say or do that would make him change his mind, Dade decided to end her doubts with another kiss.

He backed her against the wall, next to the portraits of his family, and he put his mouth to hers. Dade didn't stop there. He pressed his body against hers, until there wasn't a sliver of space between them. And he kept kissing her until he heard that sigh. That little sound of surrender and pleasure. Kayla melted against him.

"Well?" he challenged. "Got any doubts now?"

Kayla eased back, her chest pumping for air, her heart racing. "None. I love you, Dade Ryland, and more than my next breath, I want to be your wife."

Good. That's exactly what he wanted, too.

Dade smiled and pulled her back to him for another kiss. "Welcome home, Kayla."

* * * * *

Get 4 FREE REWARDS!

We'll send you 2 FREE Books plus 2 FREE Mystery Gifts.

Harlequin Special Edition books relate to finding comfort and strength in the support of loved ones and enjoying the journey no matter what life throws your way.

FREE
Value Over
$20

Get 4 FREE REWARDS!

We'll send you 2 FREE Books plus 2 FREE Mystery Gifts.

Harlequin Historical books will seduce you with passion, drama and sumptuous detail of romances set in long-ago eras!

FREE Value Over $20

Visit
ReaderService.com
Today!

As a valued member of the Harlequin Reader Service, you'll find these benefits and more at ReaderService.com:

- Try 2 free books from any series
- Access risk-free special offers
- View your account history & manage payments
- Browse the latest Bonus Bucks catalog

Don't miss out!

If you want to stay up-to-date on the latest at the Harlequin Reader Service and enjoy more content, make sure you've signed up for our monthly News & Notes email newsletter. Sign up online at ReaderService.com or by calling Customer Service at 1-800-873-8635.